AFRICAN-AMERICAN
CHILDREN'S STORIES

A TREASURY OF TRADITION AND PRIDE

Cover illustrated by
Angela Jarecki

Publications International, Ltd.

Take some of the Readings with a grain of Salt

CONTENTS

CONTENTS

CONTENTS

INTRODUCTION

The folktales contained in this treasury will take you to many interesting, exciting, and sometimes even magical places. You will come across talking animals, animals that play tricks on each other, people who can change into animals, and people who perform heroic deeds. In the last section of this book, you also will discover real-life African-Americans who have made great contributions to science, medicine, music, art, and many other fields.

America, with its mixture of people from all over the world, is very unique. The accomplishments and creativity of just one group of people, African-Americans, is showcased in this treasury. Their stories will take you on a journey into the past and then bring you up to the present day.

Some people say it is not important to read old stories. But there is so much to learn from these tales, some of which have been passed along for hundreds of years. They bring so much enjoyment that they should not be forgotten.

There is no way to determine exactly how old certain folktales and folk songs are, or even to know who created them. The slaves who were brought to America through the mid-1800s did not have many possessions, but they brought with them a rich oral tradition. This tradition has stirred the soul of America because it comes from the heart.

The history of African-Americans has been passed along in their stories, songs, and poems. This history describes the lives of people who enjoyed life as much as they could but also suffered through many hardships and struggles. Despite the difficult times they endured, most were able to display amazing courage, grace, and dignity. Many of the stories contained in this treasury convey the hopes and dreams of several generations of African-Americans.

People all over the world have heard and read the Br'er Rabbit stories. Some of the best-known African-American folktales are "told" by Uncle Remus, but Joel Chandler Harris was the actual person who collected and wrote down these stories. Harris put together the folktales he learned as a child, and his first collection was printed in 1881.

Although these tales have been controversial, they are becoming more accepted because of their place in history. In these tales, Br'er Rabbit was cunning. He outsmarted Br'er Fox and other animals time and time again. Some of the dialect, or manner of speech, of the 1800s has been kept in the stories, in which Br'er Rabbit is seen as representing slaves, with Br'er Fox representing slave owners.

Also included here are many well-known selections of African-American music. These songs tell about hardships as well as triumphs. The thought of freedom was probably never very far from the minds of slaves, and these songs were sung with a lot of feeling and emotion.

The last section of this book provides a brief look at real African-Americans whose achievements have enriched all of our lives.

What we hope to do with this treasury is to keep this wonderful heritage alive. We want to share it with our children and have them pass it on someday to their children, too.

—*Professor Gwendolyn Battle Lavert, Indiana Wesleyan University*

THE MAGIC BONES

Adapted by Yon Walls
Illustrated by Leigh Toldi

nce there were three brothers who lived in a land that was very dry and where not much food would grow. One hot day the youngest brother became sick, and the two older brothers took him under a shady tree to get well. "The baobab tree with its big leaves will heal him," they thought.

After three days and three nights the youngest brother still did not feel better. The older brothers left the sick brother all by himself. The sick brother cried, "Please don't leave me!" But they left him anyway.

One day, the youngest brother began to feel better. He made his home under the baobab tree and built a big box with branches and thorns to catch food.

He put the box near a village. When he returned the next day to see if he had caught food for dinner, he saw that an old man was trapped in the box.

"I know you are hungry," said the old man. "I have some magic bones. Throw the bones and make a wish."

The boy threw the magic bones, and suddenly cassava plants appeared. As the boy ate the tasty cassava, the old man said, "I will soon die. My name is Jambajimbira, which means 'jumping drum.' When I die, I will leave the magic bones to you. Just take the bones to a grassy field, throw them, and say my name. After you throw them you will get whatever you want." Then the old man died.

The boy found a grassy field, threw the magic bones, and called out Jambajimbira's name. Then the boy said, "Let there be a large village and plenty of food." Right before his eyes appeared a large village full of people, and there was lots of food for everyone. The villagers called the boy "Jambajimbira."

The two brothers who had left their youngest brother under the shady baobab tree heard about the chief named Jambajimbira. They traveled to his village to speak to him. "Jambajimbira, we are hungry!" they said. Jambajimbira gave each of them a bowl of milk and asked them to drink.

"Have you forgotten me?" Jambajimbira said to the two brothers. "I am your youngest brother!"

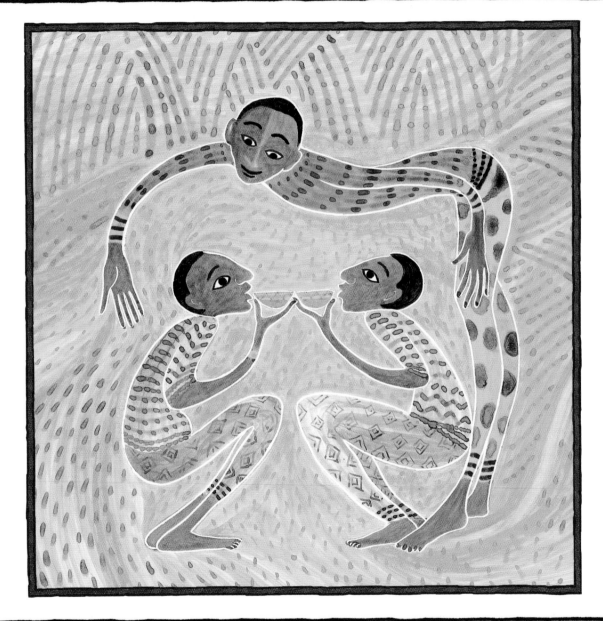

When the brothers heard Jambajimbira speak they began to cry. "Oh brother, we missed you!" they said.

Jambajimbira forgave them and said, "You can live in my village, and I will give each of you wives."

After months of living in the village, the two brothers wanted to be like Jambajimbira and rule a village. "We are the older brothers," they thought. "We should rule a fine village. If we can find the magic bones we can become chiefs."

While Jambajimbira was away from the village, the two brothers found the magic bones and wished for a village all their own. They also made their brother's village disappear.

When Jambajimbira returned and found out what his brothers had done, he started to cry. Kalib the rat and Ngabi the great hawk saw this and said, "Jambajimbira, stop crying. We will help you get back the magic bones. But what will you give us in return?"

"Anything you wish," replied Jambajimbira.

Kalib said, "I want lots of nuts," and Ngabi said, "I want chickens."

The rat ran and the hawk flew to the village of the two brothers. Kalib crawled into the largest house in the village and quietly dragged out the bones. One of the villagers saw him and shouted, "The chiefs' magic bones are being carried away by the rat!" Then Ngabi swooped down and flew away with Kalib. The villagers shouted, "Well done!" They believed the hawk would eat the rat.

But Ngabi carried Kalib and the magic bones back to Jambajimbira, who was filled with joy. Jambajimbira threw the magic bones and said, "Let there be nuts and chickens for Kalib and Ngabi."

Jambajimbira threw the bones once again and said, "Please return my village, and may the village of my two brothers disappear forever." Jambajimbira's village returned, and everyone danced with joy. The brothers' village had disappeared, and no one saw or even heard of those two brothers ever again.

NOBODY KNOWS THE TROUBLE I'VE SEEN

Nobody knows the trouble I've seen,
Nobody knows but Jesus!
Nobody knows the trouble I've seen,
Glory Hal-le-lu-jah!

Sometimes I'm up, sometimes I'm down,
Oh yes, Lord.
Sometimes I'm almost to the ground,
Oh yes, Lord.
Although you see me going along so,
Oh yes, Lord.
I have my trials here below,
Oh yes, Lord.

Nobody knows the trouble I've seen,
Nobody knows but Jesus!
Nobody knows the trouble I've seen,
Glory Hal-le-lu-jah!

HOW BR'ER RABBIT OUTSMARTED THE FROGS

Adapted by Gwendolyn Battle Lavert
Illustrated by James Hoston

Br'er Rabbit's friend, Br'er Raccoon, liked to catch frogs for his meals, so he traveled quite often down to the river with his tow sack. He would slowly sneak up behind a frog, grab him, and drop him into his sack.

One day the frogs called a great big frog meeting. They were tired of so many of their brothers and sisters being caught by Br'er Raccoon. The bullfrog said, "I will sit on the riverbank and watch for that raccoon. When he gets within half a mile of the river, I will call out to warn all of you."

The next time Br'er Raccoon went to the river, there were no frogs in sight, so he had to go back home without any frogs in his sack. When his wife saw the empty sack, she was hopping mad.

"You came back with an empty tow sack?!" yelled Br'er Raccoon's wife. Then she grabbed a broom and chased him around the house.

"Get down to that river tomorrow," she hollered, "and don't you come back without some big, fat frogs!"

Bright and early the next morning, Br'er Raccoon left the house with a big bump on his head and an empty tow sack. When he got to the river he saw his friend Br'er Rabbit, who was fishing.

"Well, howdy-do, Br'er Raccoon," said the rabbit. "How are you?"

"See this bump on my head?" said Br'er Raccoon. "My wife hit me with a broom. I can't seem to catch those wild frogs anymore."

"Well, I just think you need a plan," said Br'er Rabbit. "Next time you come to the river, fall down and play dead like Br'er Possum."

"Then what do I do?" asked Br'er Raccoon.

"You don't do anything. Just lie there and don't move till I tell you to move," said Br'er Rabbit.

"That is a wonderful plan," said Br'er Raccoon. "I don't understand it, but it is a wonderful plan."

The next day Br'er Raccoon got about half a mile from the river when he heard the bullfrog calling, "Here he comes! Here he comes! Here he comes!"

Br'er Raccoon was not worried, because he had a plan. He marched on down to the river and groaned, "Ohhhh, I'm dying of starvation. I ain't had any frogs to eat for days and days. Ooooooh, I'm dead."

Then he fell on his back, stuck his feet straight in the air, and kicked about nine times. He lay there just like he was dead. The frogs had popped their eyes up above the water and were watching him.

Br'er Rabbit came by and said, "I guess someone should dig him a grave." And the frogs said, "We can dig it! We can dig it! We can dig it!"

"Very well," said Br'er Rabbit. "Since I'm so torn up with grief and all, I guess I will let you dig it."

So all the frogs got their shovels, gathered around Br'er Raccoon, and started to dig.

They dug and dug and dug. Br'er Raccoon, who was pretending to be dead, was going further and further down in the ground, and all the frogs were going down with him. Finally, the bullfrog said, "Is the hole deep enough?"

"Well," said Br'er Rabbit, "I don't see you standing next to me, so it must be deep enough."

The bullfrog looked up and was kind of confused, especially when Br'er Rabbit yelled down to Br'er Raccoon, "Get up, Br'er Raccoon, and pick up your groceries. This hole is too deep for those wild frogs to jump out of."

So Br'er Raccoon started grabbing frogs and throwing as many of them as he could into that tow sack.

The bullfrog and all the other frogs yelled, "He tricked us! He tricked us! He tricked us!"

Well, Br'er Raccoon grabbed so many frogs that he and his wife had enough to eat for that year and the next year to boot! Br'er Raccoon's wife even stopped chasing him with a broom. And that's the end of that!

HAMBONE

Hambone, Hambone, where you been?
'Round the world and back again!

Hambone, Hambone, where's your wife?
In the kitchen cooking rice.

Hambone, Hambone, have you heard?
Papa's gonna buy me a mockingbird.

If that mockingbird don't sing
Papa's gonna buy me a diamond ring.

If that diamond ring don't shine,
Papa's gonna buy me a fishing line.

Hambone, Hambone, where you been?
'Round the world and back again!

THAT MULE WON'T WORK

Adapted by Tara Jaye Morrow
Illustrated by Ron Husband

Once upon a hot and sunny afternoon, an old man and his only grandson were resting and talking. They lived all by themselves on a big farm, where they worked and played together. The grandson was a good boy, but he was not always up to doing his share of the work.

If the grandfather asked him to go to the store for a quart of milk, the grandson would say, "I hurt my leg when I was fishing this morning." If the grandfather asked him to go out in the yard and rake the leaves, the grandson would say, "I can't find the rake."

On this day, the grandfather told the boy, "Go down to the barn, hitch up the mule, and then take him out to plow the north forty acres."

The boy was not looking forward to this job at all. The grandfather knew this, too, because he watched the boy walk real slow with his head hung low all the way down the road to the barn. What normally would be a quick trip turned out to take nearly five minutes.

When the boy finally reached the barn, the mule was standing very still with his head down in the hay. The boy thought he was eating, but that mule was watching the boy's every step.

The grandson walked right up to the old mule and said, "Come on, mule. Let's get going. Granddad says we have to plow the north forty."

The mule looked the boy straight between the eyes. Then he opened his mouth really wide, and out it came. "You tell your grandpa," snapped the mule, "that I'm not doing any work today."

The grandson jumped back, and his jaw dropped in surprise. Then he ran back home as fast as he could to find his grandfather. "Granddad!" yelled the boy. "That mule said he's not doing any work today!"

Another excuse, the grandfather thought. "You go back there and tell that mule that he WILL do his work today," said Granddad.

The boy was a little scared, but he took a deep breath and walked back to the barn. Then he looked the mule straight between his eyes and said in his biggest, strongest voice, "My granddad said you WILL do your work today."

Well, the old mule did not like that one bit. He shook his head and stamped his hooves. Dust flew everywhere, even in the boy's hair.

"You go up there," said the mule, "and tell your granddad that I said I'm NOT doing any work today! And that's it!"

The boy ran back home. When he saw his grandfather, he told him, "That mule said to tell you he's NOT doing any work today."

The grandfather figured the boy just didn't want to work. He turned to the boy and said, "Oh yeah? That does it. I'm going to tell him myself!"

The grandfather angrily picked up his cane and started down the old dirt road to the barn. The boy and their dog followed close behind.

The old man walked straight over to the mule. "Now you listen up, mule. If I say you're going to plow today, that's just what you're going to do!"

The mule snorted, kicked his leg back, and plain as day, he replied, "And I say I'm NOT going to plow today!"

The grandfather jumped back and let out a holler. Then he, the boy, and the dog ran all the way to the chopping stump before they slumped to the ground in a huff.

"I can't believe it," said the grandfather. "Who ever heard of a talking mule?"

"Not me," said the boy.

"I wouldn't have believed it if I hadn't seen it with my own two eyes," said the dog.

"I never heard of such a mess!" said the axe.

"I know that's right," said the woodpile.

"You're all losing it," said the stump.

DOWN BY THE RIVERSIDE

Gonna lay down my burden,
Down by the riverside,
Down by the riverside,
Down by the riverside.
Gonna lay down my burden,
Down by the riverside,
To study war no more.

Gonna lay down my sword and shield,
Down by the riverside,
Down by the riverside,
Down by the riverside.
Gonna lay down my sword and shield,
Down by the riverside,
To study war no more.

How It Pays Sometimes to Be Small

Adapted by Kupenda Auset
Illustrated by Cathy Johnson

Once there was a beautiful young woman whom many wanted to have as a wife. The young woman's admirers came from near and far just for the chance to marry her. One of these admirers was Sundu, the Red Antelope.

Sundu traveled to the young woman's village, where he announced to everyone that he was looking for a wife. All of the villagers thought the handsome Sundu would make a good husband, and they said to him, "We have just the right wife for you!"

Sundu spent the night in the village with hopes of meeting the young woman. When morning arrived, the young woman came to meet Sundu. After they talked for a while, she told him, "Go and get me some honey."

Off went Sundu. He found a honey tree, cut a long vine, and tied it to the tree. Sundu started to climb up toward the honey, but it was a long, long way. As big and as strong as Sundu was, he could not reach it.

Finally, Sundu gave up and returned to the village. The villagers said, "What kind of animal are you that you cannot even get your wife-to-be some honey? You are not fit to be her husband. Go, get out of here!"

So Sundu left and went back to his camp, where he told his sad story. Boloko the Ape listened and thought, "I need a wife, and I am strong and handsome. I am sure that I will win the affection of this young woman." Boloko headed straight to the village. "I hear that you have a beautiful young lady here," he said. "I know she will be very interested in marrying me."

That night, Boloko waited in the village with hopes of meeting the young woman. After they met the next morning, she said to him, "I want some honey. Go and find some for me." So Boloko went out into the woods, cut a big wood vine, and fixed it to the tree where the honey was. But when he started to climb toward the honey, he found it was much higher than he thought. As hard as he tried, Boloko could not reach the honey.

Finally, Boloko came back down without the honey. He returned to the disappointed villagers, who said to Boloko, "What kind of animal are you that you can't even bring your wife-to-be some honey? Go away right now!"

A little mouse named Makatuwa lived in the same camp as Sundu and Boloko, and he had heard all about the young woman. He thought about how much he would like someone like her to be his wife.

When little Makatuwa arrived in the village, not one villager laughed. In fact, they were very kind to him. That night, the mouse waited in the village for the chance to meet the young woman. The next morning, the young woman and the mouse met. Before the young woman could make her demand, Makatuwa told her, "I will go and get you some honey."

Makatuwa went to the forest and found a tall tree filled with honey. He cut a vine, tied it to the tree, and climbed up. The mouse worked hard to dig out all of the honey there was, and then he brought it down.

Makatuwa took the honey back to the village. "Ah!" said the villagers. "Finally, here is someone who can get honey for the woman he wants to marry."

The villagers were very happy that the mouse showed he could take care of both himself and the young woman. "Makatuwa is the husband we want for her!" shouted all of the villagers.

And so it was not the fine red antelope, nor was it the handsome ape, but it was the little mouse who earned the affection of the beautiful young woman. The young woman decided that she did, in fact, want to marry Makatuwa.

The next day, Makatuwa and the young woman were married. On that joyous day, Makatuwa knew he had learned the lesson of his life. If he believed in himself, took chances, and did his best work, he would be rewarded in more ways than he could ever imagine.

Makatuwa and his new wife lived very happily, and all of the villagers were very pleased.

Get on Board, Little Children

The Gospel train's a-comin',
I hear it just at hand.
I hear the car wheels movin',
And rumblin' through the land.

Get on board little children,
Get on board little children,
Get on board little children,
For there's room for many a more.

The fare is cheap and all can go,
The rich and poor are there.
No second-class on board the train,
No difference in the fare.

Get on board little children,
Get on board little children,
Get on board little children,
For there's room for many a more.

A Man Who Could Transform Himself

Adapted by Gino L. Morrow II
Illustrated by Sylvester Island

There once was a man named Jamal. He and his older brother Ebopp were orphans who lived together. When their parents passed away they left a few cows and several goats for the two brothers to care for.

One day Jamal said to his brother, "Let me take the goats and go to a medicine man. If I give him these goats, I am sure he will give me magical powers." Ebopp agreed that Jamal should give it a try.

Jamal traveled for several days to bring the goats to a famous medicine man in the low country. Jamal presented the goats to him, and the medicine man was so grateful that he gave Jamal magical powers. Now Jamal could transform himself into any kind of animal he wanted.

Jamal returned home and told his brother Ebopp about his new powers. Jamal then said, "If I change into an animal, don't tell anyone my secret."

Ebopp promised Jamal that he would never tell anyone about his special powers.

One day Jamal changed himself into a huge bull, and Ebopp took him to the market. Jamal and Ebopp had a secret plan. Ebopp would sell Jamal as a bull, then Jamal would run away from his buyer and change back into a human. Jamal and Ebopp would keep whatever they got from the buyer they tricked.

All of the people at the market who saw Ebopp and the bull, which was really Jamal, stopped and stared. "Where has such a big bull come from?" they all asked. One man at the market wanted to buy something wonderful, so he asked how much that big bull cost.

"This is a fine bull, so it will cost you two cows and five goats," answered Ebopp. The man happily agreed to the price and bought the bull.

The buyer planned to show off his new bull to impress the father of the woman he wanted to marry. The buyer left with the bull and headed toward his home, but before he got there the bull started to run away. The man chased after it, but he was not able to keep up.

When it was out of sight, the bull quickly changed itself so that one half looked like a lion. Then it disappeared into a dark forest.

The man followed the animal's trail. On the ground he saw the prints of a lion's paws. "It has already been taken by a lion!" the man cried out. Then he went home, feeling sad that he had lost his bull.

The animal ran on, and when it was far enough away, it changed itself back into Jamal. Jamal then returned home and saw the cows and goats that Ebopp brought back from the market that day.

The brothers played the same trick at another market the next day. Again, Jamal transformed himself into a bull. Ebopp sold him for some goats and took the goats back home. At the same time, Jamal, as the bull, was being taken to the home of the man who bought him. Jamal did not know that his new owner had also been to the medicine man and now had his own magical powers. Jamal, the bull, leaped off the man's truck and ran away.

The owner chased the bull toward the forest and very nearly caught it. That's when Jamal decided to change into a lion, thinking that the man would be scared if he saw a huge lion. But the other man also changed into a lion and kept chasing Jamal.

When Jamal saw that he was about to be caught, he changed himself into a bird and flew away. But the other man changed into a kite, and both of them flew around in the sky, with the kite chasing the bird.

Again, Jamal saw he was close to being caught. So he came down to the ground, changed himself into an antelope, and continued to run. The man chasing Jamal changed into a wolf, and the two ran on till at last Jamal stopped.

After both men changed back into human beings, Jamal said, "Okay, let's go to my house, and I'll give you back your goats." They went to Jamal's house, and Jamal and Ebopp did indeed give the goats back to the man.

Jamal had learned one thing for sure. He had met his match in making magic!

This Little Light of Mine

This little light of mine,
I'm gonna let it shine.
Oh, this little light of mine,
I'm gonna let it shine.

This little light of mine,
I'm gonna let it shine.
Let it shine,
Let it shine,
Let it shine.

This little light of mine,
I'm gonna let it shine.
Oh, this little light of mine,
I'm gonna let it shine.

The Gift and the Giver

Adapted by Kupenda Auset
Illustrated by Adjoa Burrowes

nce there was a very poor farmer who found a magnificent apple growing on a tree in his field. It was so large, so shiny, and so well-shaped that the farmer cried with joy when he saw it. In all his days, the farmer had never seen such a magnificent apple on any tree, anywhere.

The farmer picked the apple, wrapped it in his coat, and took it home. Once there, he could not wait to show it to his wife and daughter. When he uncovered the apple in front of them, they were as amazed at it as he was.

They all wondered what should be done with the apple. The farmer wanted to give it to his daughter, so he told her, "This is truly the only thing that matches you in beauty. I want you to take this apple, eat it, and enjoy it."

But the daughter was modest, and she told her father that he should keep the apple for himself. She believed that the apple had been given to her father as a sign of God's love and blessings. "It is worthy of a king," the daughter said, complimenting her father.

"You are right," the farmer said, thinking of their king instead. "Such a perfect piece of fruit is worthy of a king. It is the only gift that I, a poor farmer, can give that would be worthy of our king."

The farmer soon left for the royal city. After many days he reached the city, but when he got to the palace, the poor farmer could not get in to see the king. The palace guards laughed at him and would not let him in.

"The king has thousands of fruit trees," said one of the guards. "We are sure that your apple cannot be any more beautiful than the ones the king already has."

The farmer asked the guards to look more closely at what he had brought. The apple was still as beautiful as it had been the day he had picked it.

Finally, a guard called for his commander to look at the apple. The commander was very impressed. He admired the apple as much as the farmer did, so he decided to bring the farmer to the king's chambers.

When the farmer came before the king, he said, "Your Majesty, I have found an extraordinary apple. I decided that only you are deserving of this apple."

The king was deeply moved by the farmer's gift. "What would you accept from me in return?" the king asked.

The farmer was very surprised by the question. "I want nothing, Your Majesty, but to see the joy on your face when you see this apple that God has made," the farmer said.

While people in the palace were admiring the apple, the poor farmer left to return home. "Where is the farmer?" the king asked. "He has shown me more love with this gift than anyone in the kingdom. Go find him. Take my finest horse and give it to him."

They went after the farmer and found him. The farmer looked tired, and was walking slowly along the road. When the servants gave the farmer the horse, he was surprised and overjoyed with the King's gift and rode away happily toward his village.

Soon, a rich merchant of the city heard the story of the king's gift and immediately began to scheme. "What could I get from the king if I gave him my best horse?" thought the merchant. "Perhaps some valuable jewels!"

The merchant brought his best horse to the palace. The merchant went to the king and said, "I have brought you the finest horse from my stable."

"Ah, I see," said the king. "You have given me a gift. Now you expect something in return. All right. Take this apple. It is so precious to me because it was given by a man who expected nothing in return. You may have it."

The merchant angrily threw the apple away. The king ordered his guards to remove the merchant from the palace grounds. "Tell him," the king said, "that a gift is only as good as the heart of the giver. A person should give without expecting a gift in return. Any other gift is of no value. This horse is worthless as a gift because of the greedy heart of the merchant. As something to ride on, however, it seems to be a very fine horse."

KUM BA YAH

Kum ba yah my Lord,
Kum ba yah!
Kum ba yah my Lord,
Kum ba yah!
Kum ba yah my Lord,
Kum ba yah!
Oh Lord, Kum ba yah.

Someone's crying, Lord,
Kum ba yah!
Someone's singing, Lord,
Kum ba yah!
Someone's praying, Lord,
Kum ba yah!
Oh Lord, Kum ba yah.

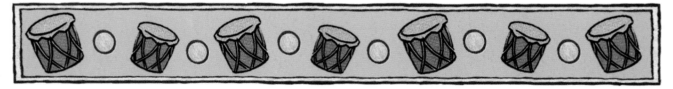

Two Ways to Count to Ten

Adapted by Yon Walls
Illustrated by Leigh Toldi

The people in the village were very excited. "Tanko the great storyteller is coming!" they shouted. Men, women, and children ran to greet him. They all gathered in the biggest hut to hear Tanko's story. There was a place for everyone to sit.

Tanko appeared in a large yellow robe. He greeted the people by singing a song. "Ai Ei!" the notes rang out. To welcome Tanko as a guest, the villagers made him a large bowl of yams. After he finished eating the yams, he sat quietly on the floor of the hut.

Tanko then took a small drum out of his big bag, which was made from tiger's skin. He began to tap on the drum, *tita, tita, tita*. Everyone loved the sound of the drum. "What story will you tell?" asked an elder in the village.

"I will tell the story of the great King Leopard," said Tanko. And that is when he began to tell his unusual tale.

Long ago in the land of animals, there were tribes of animals that lived together in harmony.

All the animals could talk, and there was a king who ruled over them. The king had a very beautiful daughter, the Leopard Princess. All the animals obeyed the king.

One day, King Leopard said, "Who will rule the animal kingdom when I am gone? I must find someone who is wise and compassionate. He will also marry my pretty daughter, the Leopard Princess."

After King Leopard made his announcement, he had a great feast. Everyone danced and ate okra and rice. After the dancing and eating, the guests gathered in a circle. King Leopard told them, "To become the prince and to marry my daughter, the smartest beast must throw a spear into the air and count to ten before it falls." Everyone whispered, "Oh, who will be prince?"

Many beasts in the jungle wanted to throw the spear to become prince and to marry King Leopard's pretty daughter. The first to throw the king's spear was the elephant. The elephant was the biggest and strongest beast in the jungle.

"I will throw the king's spear the highest and count to ten before it lands," the elephant shouted. But he was too clumsy, and his body was heavy. When he threw the spear into the sky, he only counted, "One, two, three," before the king's spear landed on the ground. The elephant was very embarrassed. He had lost the contest.

The next beast to throw the spear was the water ox. "I will throw the king's spear higher than ten mango trees!" he shouted. The water ox threw the spear with his horns and quickly counted, "One, two, three, four." But then the king's spear landed with a thump. The ox had lost the contest, too.

Then it was the chimpanzee's turn. With his long arms he threw the spear. "One, two, three, four, five, six, seven," he shouted. But the spear landed in the king's vegetable garden. The chimpanzee lost the contest. The villagers began to whisper, "Who will marry the king's daughter?"

Then out of the bush came a beast no one had seen before. It was the antelope, with large eyes and slender legs. "He is not strong enough to throw the spear," said the villagers.

"I will throw the spear," the antelope said with courage to the King.

The antelope walked lightly and was very graceful. With very little effort, he threw the King's spear high into the sky and called out two words, "Five, ten!"

"I have counted to ten," said the antelope proudly.

The king nodded his head and said, "Yes, you have counted to ten. I did not say how you must count to ten."

The king then told the antelope, "You will be the prince and will marry my daughter." The other animals felt sad that they were not smart enough to be prince.

After three days of dancing and feasting, King Leopard announced, "Antelope is the new prince," and all the beasts shouted for joy.

Everyone in the land was happy because they realized that it is not always the biggest or strongest, but the smartest one who wins the prize.

DOWN IN MY HEART

I've got that joy, joy, joy, joy,
Down in my heart,
Down in my heart,
Down in my heart!

I've got that joy, joy, joy, joy,
Down in my heart,
Down in my heart today!

I've got that love of Jesus
Down in my heart,
Down in my heart,
Down in my heart!

I've got that love of Jesus
Down in my heart,
Down in my heart today!

Good Blanche, Bad Rose, and the Magic Eggs

Adapted by Eleanor Engram
Illustrated by Joey Hart

Two beautiful little girls, Blanche and Rose, lived with their mother at the edge of a very dark and mysterious forest. "Rose, you look just like me," their mother often said. Rose thought this meant she was grown, so she did just what she wanted and refused to help with the chores.

One day while their mother was sweeping the floor, she said, "Girls, we need some water. Please go out to the well and fill the bucket." Blanche jumped up, glad to go to the well, but Rose, pretending she did not hear her mother, sat rocking in her chair, playing with her bear.

Blanche went to the well and let her bucket down to get some water. Out of nowhere an old woman appeared. "Come here, little girl," she said, "and give me a drink of water." Blanche was a bit scared, but then she remembered that she always obeyed her elders, so she gave the old woman a drink of water.

"You are a good girl," the old woman said, and then she disappeared into thin air.

When Blanche went back to the well the next day, the old woman came again. "Follow me," the woman said. "You'll be safe."

Blanche followed the old woman deep into the forest. Startled by a noise, she turned, and right in front of her were two axe heads battling. "This is very strange," Blanche said, hurrying to get around them. Just then, out of nowhere, came two arms boxing each other. Blanche was afraid, but the old woman just laughed and said, "Come on, you are a good little girl!"

Just when Blanche thought she had all she could take, right in front of her, hanging in the middle of the air, were two witches riding on broomsticks. Blanche was terrified. She followed the old woman into the cabin and watched as the woman put a bone into a pot of water that was boiling inside the fireplace. The woman then put the pot on a table.

Blanche watched as the pot filled with a thick stew of meat, potatoes, and gravy. She turned in amazement to see the old woman and her chair begin to rise off the floor!

The old woman floated closer to Blanche. "Go in the back to the chicken house," she told Blanche, "and there you will find eggs that talk. Some will say, 'Take me.' Some will say, 'Don't take me.'"

The old woman continued, "If you do what they say, by the time you get home, you will have gold and diamonds and beautiful clothes."

Blanche did just what the eggs said. She filled her apron with eggs that said, "Take me," and sure enough, by the time she got home, her arms were filled with treasures.

Blanche's mother was very happy to learn about the old woman and the talking eggs. She turned to Rose. "Go," she said, "and bring back more riches than Blanche brought."

Rose hurried to the forest to look for the old woman. She passed the battling axes. She passed the boxing arms and then the flying witches. At last Rose came to the cabin, but she went straight to the chicken house. Some eggs were calling, "Take me!" and others were calling, "Don't take me!"

Rose did something very bad. Every time an egg said, "Don't take me," she grabbed it and put it in her apron. Rose said to herself, "If Blanche got all that by being good, I can get much more by being bad! I won't let those talking eggs fool me!"

Rose went back through the forest. The axes stopped fighting and chased after her. One of the boxing arms tried to grab her, and a flying witch just missed crashing into her. The eggs cracked open, and toads came out, crawling into her hair, into her pockets, and into the hem of her dress. Snakes crawled from other eggs and chased Rose back to her house. Her mother met her at the door. Snakes, toads, and all kinds of ugly creatures followed Rose into the house.

"Get out of here, Bad Rose," her mother cried as she chased Rose, the snakes, and the toads straight through the house and into the backyard.

Rose ran into their chicken house. "You will sleep there from now on, you disobedient child!" her mother cried. And Bad Rose really did spend every night in the chicken house.

I'M GOING HOME

I sought my Lord in the wilderness,
In the wilderness, in the wilderness.
I sought my Lord in the wilderness,
    For I am going home.

    For I am going home,
    For I am going home,
    I'm just getting ready,
    For I am going home.

I found free grace in the wilderness,
In the wilderness, in the wilderness.
I found free grace in the wilderness,
    For I am going home.

    For I am going home,
    For I am going home,
    I'm just getting ready,
    For I am going home.

Jackal's Favorite Game

Adapted by Gale Greenlee
Illustrated by Eric Wilkerson

ackal was a sorry friend. Every day, he'd meet Hare by the lake to play forest games. But being a poor sport and a very selfish creature, Jackal always insisted on having his way. Even when Hare was not in the mood for games, Jackal would chase him and tease him and tickle Hare until he agreed to play.

"But I don't want to play," Hare often complained.

"Sure you do," Jackal would always say with a laugh, as he tackled Hare and they both rolled on the ground.

Today, it was happening again. "Let me go!" squealed Hare, as Jackal tickled him. "Let me go!"

"Not until you say you'll play," Jackal said, and he tickled Hare some more.

"Okay, hee hee, I give! I give!" chuckled Hare. "We can play hide-and-seek."

Now, that was Jackal's favorite game. So he always shouted, "You're it, Hare! I hide first!"

Then Jackal ran off into the woods, leaving Hare to count. And that's how things always worked between Jackal and Hare . . . until things changed.

One morning, Hare headed down to the river to play by himself, singing a little song as he went:

> I can bounce and jump,
>> Hop and bump.
>>> I can sing and fly,
>>>> And touch the sky!

Then Hare heard a laugh, and he knew it was Jackal. "I know you're there," Jackal said. Hare walked up to Jackal and insisted he would not play with him if Jackal tickled and teased him so.

"All right," Jackal agreed. "But I'll hide first, because I'm bigger and older than you, and this is my favorite game." Since this was true, Hare counted once again. After a while, Hare finally got his chance to hide. As Jackal began to count, Hare bounced off in search of a good hiding place.

Hare jumped deeper and deeper into the forest and stumbled upon a small cave. The cave was the perfect spot to hide, covered by leaves and blocked by trees.

"Jackal will never find me here," thought Hare.

"Okay, here I come," Jackal said as he started the search for his friend. He looked behind small rocks and big rocks, behind bushes and up tall trees.

As Jackal walked deeper into the forest, he pushed away tree limbs and other plants and finally saw the entrance to the cave. He peeked in for just a second, and what did he see? Looking back at him were two enormous green eyes!

"A beast! A beast!" screamed Jackal. Then he ran off as quickly as he could.

"That's not like Jackal," thought Hare. "He loves this game. Why'd he leave so quickly? And who is this beast?"

Hare hopped off after Jackal. Jackal soon heard the sound of someone running behind him.

"Oh no! The beast is after me!" cried Jackal. "The beast is going to eat me!" Jackal quickly hid behind a large rock, shaking with fear.

Hare walked up to the rock. "Jackal, come out," he said.

"Please don't hurt me, Mister Monster," pleaded Jackal.

"Oh Jackal, it's me. Look!" insisted Hare.

Jackal looked up and saw Hare's enormous green eyes. "That was you in the cave?" Jackal asked.

"Yep," said Hare with a laugh.

"Oh, your eyes scared me," Jackal said. "I thought you were a beast! Please don't ever do that again."

"I won't scare you if you promise to be a better sport and a better friend," replied Hare.

"It's a deal," said Jackal. Then they shook hands and decided to play another game. This time, Hare went first, and he was very happy.

TAKE THIS HAMMER

Take this hammer,
Carry it to the captain.
Take this hammer,
Carry it to the captain.
Take this hammer,
Carry it to the captain.
Tell him I'm gone,
Tell him I'm gone.

If he asks you
Was I running,
If he asks you
Was I running,
If he asks you
Was I running,
Tell him I was flying,
Tell him I was flying.

MALAIKA AND BR'ER RABBIT

Adapted by Gwendolyn Battle Lavert
Illustrated by Beverly Hawkins Hall

Malaika cried when her mama went to the market to sell vegetables. Malaika hated minding the house and garden all alone, because then she had very little time to play. Mama told her, "You have to stay here and pick the peas from our garden."

As soon as Mama left, Malaika went to her swing to play for a few minutes. Br'er Rabbit, who heard what Mama told Malaika, popped up and said, "I can pick peas for you. Keep on playing, Malaika. Have fun!"

Malaika gave Br'er Rabbit a big basket and let him into the garden. When Malaika went back to her swing, Br'er Rabbit ate a whole row of sweet, tender peas in a minute. His full belly shook. His ears, tail, and big old feet wobbled.

Malaika came back after a while, let Br'er Rabbit out of the garden, and went back to swinging. When Mama came home from the market, Malaika was still swinging high and low. "Mama," she said. "A wonderful rabbit came by, and he picked the peas. I got to play all day!"

Malaika's mama took her over to the garden and showed her that Br'er Rabbit was not so wonderful. He had eaten all the peas. The basket was empty.

"If he comes back again," said Mama, "I want you to let him in and lock the gate. Your daddy will take care of Mister Br'er Rabbit."

The next day, Br'er Rabbit hopped on over to Malaika's house. "Hey, Malaika," he said. "This sure is a fine day to play in the sun. I will pick the peas for you. Go on and swing high and low."

Malaika stayed quiet, but she opened the gate for Br'er Rabbit. He hopped inside. White puffy tail, big old feet, flippity-flop he went.

Malaika locked the gate behind Br'er Rabbit. Up and down the sweet-pea row, ears just waving, Br'er Rabbit stayed all day. Then, really late, he dragged his full belly to the gate. It was almost time for Malaika's daddy to come home from work, too. But Br'er Rabbit didn't know a thing about it.

Br'er Rabbit called, "Malaika, let me out now! I am all finished picking peas."

Malaika stopped swinging and went to the garden gate. "Br'er Rabbit, can't you see that I'm playing? I love to swing high and low. Sometimes I almost touch the blue sky. I can't be bothered with you."

Malaika's daddy came home and saw what was in the garden. Br'er Rabbit, that's what — all ears, puffy tail, and big feet. "What are you doing?" asked Daddy.

Br'er Rabbit said, "Malaika let me in here, sir."

"I see what you're up to," said Daddy. "Now, I've got something better than pea pods for you."

Br'er Rabbit hopped to the gate, flippity-flop. Malaika and her daddy grabbed him by the ears and stuffed him in a gunnysack. They hung the sack in the wild honey-locust tree and left. Soon Mister Wolf came along. He heard Br'er Rabbit coughing in the gunnysack. "Is that you, Br'er Rabbit? What are you doing in there?"

"Oh," said Br'er Rabbit. "I'm on my way to heaven for Miss Malaika. She is such a dear, sweet angel. Do you want to come?"

"Yes, indeed!" said Mister Wolf.

"Then open this gunnysack and come on in!" said Br'er Rabbit. So Mister Wolf jumped right in. Br'er Rabbit jumped right out and tied the wolf in the gunnysack. Br'er Rabbit was gone as fast as he could go. Malaika and her daddy came back and looked inside the sack.

"Mister Wolf," said Malaika, "what are you doing in there?" Malaika and her daddy laughed and let the wolf out. Then Malaika said, "When you see a gunnysack again, Mister Wolf, you'd better run as fast as you can."

Malaika added, "Make sure that Br'er Rabbit doesn't hide a trick in it, too!"

Now when Malaika goes to the market with her mama, she tells everybody, "I go around the bend. I see a fence to mend. On it is hung my story end."

MISS MARY MACK

Miss Mary Mack, Mack, Mack,
All dressed in black, black, black,
With silver buttons, buttons, buttons,
All down her back, back, back.

She asked her mother, mother, mother,
For fifteen cents, cents, cents,
To see the elephant, elephant, elephant,
Jump over the fence, fence, fence.

He jumped so high, high, high,
He almost reached the sky, sky, sky,
And he didn't come back, back, back,
Until the Fourth of July, 'ly, 'ly.

TORTOISE, HARE, AND THE SWEET POTATOES

Adapted by Gale Greenlee
Illustrated by Angela Jarecki

s long as anyone remembered, Hare always had been a shady character, forever up to no good. He spent his days telling riddles no one could answer and playing pranks on the other animals in the forest. And each night Hare thought of more new riddles and tricks he could play.

"I am the number one trickster," Hare said with a grin. "No one is more clever than me."

Tortoise, unlike Hare, was a kind-hearted creature. Each morning, she rose with the sun and happily began her daily chore of cleaning her teeny-weeny pond. She took pride in her housekeeping skills and kept the pond in tip-top shape, just in case a weary traveler ever needed a cool drink.

So Tortoise was not surprised when Hare dropped by one unusually hot autumn day. But being a friend of most forest creatures, Tortoise had heard of Hare's bad reputation. As Hare filled his cup with water, Tortoise thought, "Hare may be a swindler, but he won't fool me. I will never fall for his trickery."

All afternoon Hare tried his best to trick Tortoise. He told her his most difficult riddles, and she easily answered them. "This is harder than I imagined," Hare thought, so he tried something new.

"Miss Tortoise, please join me for lunch today," Hare asked sweetly.

"Mister Hare, we're nowhere near your home," Tortoise said, "and I have nothing in my cupboard."

"No problem," said Hare. "I know a field full of sweet potatoes ready for harvest. Let's go there."

Tortoise knew the field belonged to a mean old farmer. She did not care for the farmer, but she still thought stealing was wrong. She told Hare she would not go with him. But soon, her stomach began to grumble and growl. When Hare asked her again, she agreed, but with her own plan in mind.

Within minutes, they stepped into a giant sweet-potato patch. They pulled up sweet potatoes until their sack was full, then they built a fire and roasted the potatoes.

As Tortoise bit into a freshly roasted sweet potato, Hare said, "Hold on. What if the farmer catches us?"

Tortoise seemed unconcerned and continued to eat. She smacked her lips and said, "Oooh, this is good!"

"Shhh! Did you hear that?" said Hare. "We should check out the place and make sure it's safe!"

The two split up and went off in different directions. But Tortoise knew Hare was sneaky. When Hare was out of sight, she crawled into the sack to eat another potato in peace.

"Mmm, yummy!" Tortoise exclaimed. "I'll have just one more."

Before she could have another helping, sweet potatoes tumbled down all around her. It was Hare. He picked up the sack, flung it over his shoulder, and sprinted off hoping to leave Tortoise behind. "She'll never find me," he said.

"Boy, will Hare be surprised," Tortoise thought as she ate another sweet potato inside the sack.

After a while, Hare found a swimming hole. "Now I can drink some water, eat all the sweet potatoes, and not worry about Little Miss Slowpoke," he thought. Hare reached into the bag without looking, and Tortoise placed one of the last sweet potatoes in the hungry Hare's hand.

"Oh no," Hare thought. "Surely I can do better than this pitiful thing." Hare propped the bag up against a tree and put his hand back in, fishing around until he touched something big and warm.

"This will be a feast," Hare said. But much to his surprise, he did not pull out a sweet potato.

"Miss Tortoise!" he screamed as she rose from the sack, handing him the last pebble-sized sweet potato.

Then Tortoise grinned and said, "You may be a swindler, but you can't fool me. I'll never fall for your trickery."

Disappointed that his trick backfired, Hare cried and cried. As for Tortoise, she headed back to her pond, pleased with herself for fooling the forest's most famous trickster.

ROLL, JORDAN, ROLL

Roll, Jordan, roll,
Roll, Jordan, roll.
I want to go to heaven when I die,
To hear Jordan roll.
Oh brothers, you ought to have been there,
Yes, my Lord!
A-sitting in the Kingdom,
To hear Jordan roll.
Oh preachers, you ought to have been there,
Yes, my Lord!
A-sitting in the Kingdom,
To hear Jordan roll.
Roll, Jordan, roll,
Roll, Jordan, roll.
I want to go to heaven when I die,
To hear Jordan roll.

Hen and Frog

Adapted by Nancy Tolson
Illustrated by Michael Hobbs

Hen and Frog were traveling down the same road. Frog was flicking flies with his tongue, while Hen was pecking the ground in search of seeds to eat. Hen pecked, stepped, and flapped her wings. Each time she looked up she noticed more dark clouds in the sky.

"Oh dear," clucked Hen. "The clouds are dark and are moving this way. A storm is coming soon."

Frog flicked at a fly and slurped it down, then continued to hop down the road. "Did you hear me, Frog?" clucked Hen. "There is a storm coming soon, and we will be caught in it."

"Those clouds are not close," said Frog. "By the time the rain comes we will be home."

Hen knew Frog was wrong. She knew she must build a house to protect them from the coming storm. Hen was known as one of the best builders, and she quickly started to gather straw to start the job. "Frog, help me build this house so that we can be safe and dry from the storm," Hen clucked.

"No indeed," Frog croaked. "I do not need to build a house because of a few drops of water. Besides, here is a hole that I will sit in if the rain comes."

Hen built a very nice house. It had a window and also a fireplace to keep her warm. Since the storm had not yet come, Hen decided to make a bed.

"Frog, help me make a bed to rest on just in case the storm is a long one," Hen clucked.

"No indeed," Frog croaked. "I do not need a bed. The ground is all that I need to lie on when that little bit of rain comes our way."

Hen finished the bed and knew she would get hungry during the storm.

"Frog, help me gather some mangoes so there will be plenty to eat when the storm comes," clucked Hen.

"No indeed," Frog croaked. "I do not need mangoes when there are plenty of bugs and flies to eat."

Hen gathered lots of mangoes and placed them beneath the bed to stay dry. And then the storm began.

Rain poured down,
    Upon the ground.
        Water everywhere,
            Frog doesn't care.
                Or does he?

Frog's hole filled up with water. He quickly hopped to Hen's house. "Hen, let me in!" Frog croaked.

"No, Frog, you didn't help me build it!" clucked Hen.

"I will not call Cat if you let me in," Frog croaked. Hen was very afraid of Cat, so she quickly let Frog in. "Hen, I am tired. Let me rest on the bed," croaked Frog.

"No, Frog, you didn't help me build it," clucked Hen.

"I will not call Cat if you let me lie on the bed," Frog croaked. So Hen let Frog lie on her bed.

"Hen, I am hungry," croaked Frog. "Let me have a mango."

"No, Frog, you didn't help me pick them," clucked Hen.

"I will not call Cat if you let me eat one," Frog croaked.

Hen was getting mad at Frog. "The mangoes are on the roof. If you go get them, I will peel them for you."

Frog loved mangoes. He quickly hopped straight to the roof, but there was not a mango in sight. "Hen! Where are the mangoes?" croaked Frog.

Hen was sitting upon her bed pecking into a mango. "I have them, Frog, and you cannot have one," clucked Hen.

"Hen, If you do not give me a mango I will . . . ." Then suddenly, Hawk swooped down upon Hen's roof and took Frog away. Hen looked out her window and saw Hawk flying away with Frog.

"Cluckity cluck cluck,
        Now my work is done.
            The storm is almost over,
                And soon there will be sun!"

Standin' in the Need of Prayer

It's me, it's me, O Lord,
Standin' in the need of prayer.
It's me, it's me, O Lord,
Standin' in the need of prayer.

Not my brother, not my sister,
But it's me, O Lord,
Standin' in the need of prayer.
Not my brother, not my sister,
But it's me, O Lord,
Standin' in the need of prayer.

Not my father, not my mother,
But it's me, O Lord,
Standin' in the need of prayer.
Not my father, not my mother,
But it's me, O Lord,
Standin' in the need of prayer.

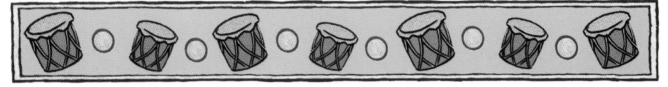

THE SON OF WIND

Adapted by Nancy Tolson
Illustrated by Felicia Marshall

nce, up on a hill where the antelopes grazed, there sat a large round hut where Mother Wind and her son lived. Son of Wind was very sad because he had no one to play with. He would look out the window at the antelopes at play and blow a secret wish across the hills. Son of Wind always wished for a playmate.

One day a boy did come up the hill, and Son of Wind was peeping out his window at the same time. "Hooraaah!" yelled Son of Wind. His secret wish had come true. Son of Wind ran out with his ball to play with the boy.

"Oh Danso!" called out Son of Wind as he threw the ball. "Catch!"

Danso looked surprised that this boy knew his name, but it was not as important as a game of catch. Danso did not know that wherever the wind blows, it hears all the names of the people.

"Here friend, catch!" said Danso as he threw the ball back to Son of Wind.

Danso and Son of Wind played all day. The two of them laughed as they tossed the ball with delight, until Mother Wind came out to call her son home. Danso tried to listen for his friend's name as his mother called, but all he heard was the whistling of the wind instead.

"Danso! When will you be back to play ball with me?" asked Son of Wind.

"I will be here tomorrow," said Danso.

Son of Wind was happy. He waved good-bye as he and his mother walked inside their hut. Danso ran home to tell his mother about his new friend. "Mother, can you tell me the name of the boy who lives in the big round hut on the hill?"

Danso's mother said, "I will tell you his name after your father has finished the wind shelter for our hut."

So each day Danso would run up the hill to play catch with his new friend, and each day when he returned home he would check to see if his father was finished making the wind shelter.

Danso wondered why he could never hear his friend's name when his mother called him home. He would only hear the "woooshin" of the wind.

Danso's father now was close to finishing the wind shelter. "Mother, can you tell me the name of my friend now?" asked Danso.

"I will tell you," said Danso's mother, "but you must promise not to say his name until you see your father resting in his chair. Then you will know the wind shelter is done. And you must promise that when you say his name you will run as fast as you can back to our hut, because there will be a mighty wind behind you."

"I promise," said Danso.

"It is Woooshin-Woooshin-Shooowaaaa-Wooosh," said Danso's mother.

So the next day Danso went to play catch on the hill. He kept his promise until he saw his father resting in a chair. "Danso, catch," Son of Wind called out.

"Catch, Woooshin-Woooshin-Shooowaaaa–Wooosh," Danso called as he threw the ball back.

Son of Wind was so surprised to hear his real name that he stumbled and fell down. He rolled and tossed in the grass, and a fierce wind began to blow. Danso started to run home, then he turned back and saw a large wind ball rolling down the hill behind him.

Danso ran faster until he reached his hut. He ran inside and shut the door. The wind ball arrived, but Danso was safe now. Woooshin-Woooshin-Shooowaaaa–Wooosh!

> When the wind wants to play
> A game of catch with you,
> Play back with the wind,
> But whatever you do,
> Don't call him by name,
> Just call him your friend,
> 'Cause you just might end up
> With a mighty fierce wind.
> Keep that name to yourself!

Go Tell It
On The Mountain

Go tell it on the mountain,
Over the hills and everywhere.
Go tell it on the mountain,
That Jesus Christ is born.

The shepherds feared and trembled,
When lo! above the earth,
Rang out the angel chorus,
That hailed our Saviour's birth.

Go tell it on the mountain,
Over the hills and everywhere.
Go tell it on the mountain,
That Jesus Christ is born.

Why Frog and Snake Never Play Together

Adapted by Renée Deshommes
Illustrated by Aaron Boyd

a Frog and Ma Snake had little girls, and both girls wanted to go out to play one sunny afternoon. Ma Snake said, "Look out for things with big paws and shiny claws. Be careful in the bush, little one, and be home before dark."

The young snake sang as she slithered through the grass, "Sssss, look out for Paws-and-Claws, sssss."

Nearby, Ma Frog called out, "Be wary of things that poke or snap. Don't wander into the bush alone, my child, and be home before sundown."

The young frog sang as she hopped away, "Rrrribit, be wary of the Poke-or-Snap, rrrribit."

Snake and Frog were still singing when they met along the way, and they almost bumped into each other. A surprised Frog asked Snake, "Are you a Poke-or-Snap?"

"Oh no," Snake said with a laugh. "Of course not! I'm a snake, and I slip and slide. Are you a Paws-and-Claws?"

"Goodness no!" replied Frog, who also laughed. "I'm a Frog. I hop and plop."

As Frog and Snake wandered together into the bush, they decided to become friends. They hugged and sang:

"Let's make a wish,
   and hope it comes true,
      to be friends forever,
         me and you."

Frog and Snake snacked on fruitflies and crunchy bugs. Frog showed Snake how to hop. "Watch me!" she said as she hopped up, up in the air and came down with a PLOP! Snake tried to hop but ended up getting in quite a tangle on the ground. Then Snake showed Frog how to slither. She went to the top of a mound and slid down — SWOOSH! Frog tried to slide but came down in a clumsy tumble.

Frog and Snake laughed at their mistakes. Dusk arrived soon after, and they knew it was time to go home. "Let's play again tomorrow," said Frog. "After all, we're friends now."

"Yes we are," replied Snake. "I will see you tomorrow." They hugged again and said goodbye.

When Frog came home, her mother was surprised to see her covered with grass. "What happened?" she asked.

Frog replied, "Oh, I had such a fun day. I met a snake, and we played together. She taught me to slide, and now we are best friends."

Ma Frog was horrified. "A snake? Dear child, don't you know that snakes eat frogs? Snakes are bad, and you must promise me that you will never play with snakes again."

Frog shivered. "Yes," she answered. "I understand."

Nearby, Snake arrived home. Ma Snake said, "My, my. You look tired. Where have you been?"

Snake happily replied, "I have a new friend named Frog. We played, and she showed me how to hop."

Ma Snake was shocked, "A frog? Little one, you are a snake, and snakes are supposed to eat frogs!"

Ma snake continued, "The next time you see her, you must gobble her up."

Snake lowered her head and answered, "Yes, Mama. I understand." The next day Snake went to Frog's house and called out, "Frog, let's play together!"

Frog huddled inside her house. "Ha!" she said. "My mother told me how snakes really like to play. No thanks. I'm going to stay right here where I'll be safe."

"Ah," snake said. "My mother talked to me too, and she told me all about frogs and what I should do."

Snake continued, "So, I guess there is nothing more to say but goodbye."

"Farewell," said Frog.

Frog and Snake never played with each other again. However, they always sadly wondered if things could have been different if only they had kept playing. If you look carefully, you might see them sitting very quietly in the sun thinking of their fun day and the promise they once sang to each other:

"Let's make a wish,
  and hope it comes true,
    to be friends forever,
      me and you."

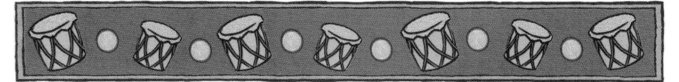

I Heard from Heaven Today

Hurry on, my weary soul,
And I heard from heaven today.
Hurry on, my weary soul,
And I heard from heaven today.

My sin is forgiven and my soul set free,
And I heard from heaven today.
My sin is forgiven and my soul set free,
And I heard from heaven today.

A baby born in Bethlehem,
And I heard from heaven today.
A baby born in Bethlehem,
And I heard from heaven today.

My name is called and I must go,
And I heard from heaven today.
My name is called and I must go,
And I heard from heaven today.

THE COMING OF NIGHT

Adapted by Renée Deshommes
Illustrated by John Patterson

Long ago, when the Earth was new, the sun always shined. There was no nighttime. No twinkling stars or golden moon. No owls sighing, "Whoo." No buzzing insects, and no leopards growling in the still of night.

The people did not know when to awaken because there was no dawn, and there was no dusk to tell them when to go to sleep. Sunlight filled the skies all the time.

Then one day Yemoya, the magical goddess of the river, sent her daughter Aje to wed Oduduwa, the Earth chief. Aje left her cool and shady home deep within the river and came to the surface.

Aje and Oduduwa soon were married. Aje loved her new home and husband, but as time passed she began to grow weary of the bright, hot sun. "Oh, how I miss the dark, cool waters of the river," Aje said. "I wish Night was here!"

Oduduwa wanted his bride to be happy, so he asked, "What is Night? Where can we find it?"

"Night is a cool, crisp sheet that covers the day's warm bed," responded Aje. "It calms all who are weary, but Night can only be found beneath the water in my mother's home."

Aje and Oduduwa decided to summon Crocodile and Hippopotamus, the river's messengers. Aje wrote a note to her mother asking her to send Night to the surface. She gave the note to the messengers.

Crocodile and Hippopotamus swam deep beneath the water until finally they arrived at Yemoya's beautiful river palace. Yemoya read the note from Aje and began to fill a sack full of the mysterious Night for the messengers to bring back to Earth.

"Careful," Yemoya warned them. "Do not open the sack. Only Aje can control the Night spirits."

Crocodile and Hippopotamus nodded, bowed, and then swam away with the sack. Once they reached the shore, they stopped to rest. Suddenly, a strange noise could be heard coming from the sack. It was the Night spirits!

"Let's open it," said Crocodile. They used their teeth to untie the knot, then . . . WHOOSH, CRICKETY-CRICK! Out hopped the night insects, all of the spiders and crickets.

WHOOSH, WHOOO, CHIRP! Out flew the night birds, all of the owls and nightingales.

WHOOSH, GRRRRR, ROARRR! Out rushed the night animals, all of the lions and leopards. Night so terrified Hippopotamus and Crocodile that they jumped in the water and swam away.

Aje had been waiting nearby. When she heard the noises, she knew just what to do. She closed her eyes, raised her hands, and hummed a soothing lullaby. At once, the Night spirits hushed, and all was peaceful across the land.

The insects scattered throughout the bush. The stars twinkled while the moonbeams glowed. The night birds nestled in the trees, and the night animals rested in the grass. A cool breeze blew in the night air. Aje had restored calm. Then she gave directions to balance Night and Day.

Aje smiled and soon fell fast asleep. Now that Night had arrived, Aje could at last be comfortable in her new home. Oduduwa was pleased that his wife was truly happy and had helped to bring the wonderful Night to Earth.

The people of Earth were happy with Night as well, and they welcomed the darkness, calm breezes, and mysterious sounds of the night creatures.

The next day, Aje decided to bring order to the land so there would always be a daytime and a nighttime.

Aje named the sun Morningstar and said, "Your job is to rise and begin the day."

She told the rooster, "You are the guardian of Night, and you shall crow to tell us when dawn is near." Aje also instructed the other birds to chirp sweetly at daybreak to help awaken all of the people.

And ever since then, the sun, rooster, and birds announce each new day, but only after the night has passed and all have had a restful sleep.

DON'T BE WEARY, TRAVELER

Don't be weary, traveler,
Come along home to Jesus!
Don't be weary, traveler,
Come along home to Jesus!

My head got wet with the midnight dew,
Come along home to Jesus!
Angels bear me witness, too,
Come along home to Jesus!

Where to go I did not know,
Come along home to Jesus!
Ever since he freed my soul,
Come along home to Jesus!

I looked at the world and the world looked new,
Come along home to Jesus!
I looked at the world and the world looked new,
Come along home to Jesus!

THE DAUGHTER OF THE SUN AND THE MOON

Adapted by Nicole Blades
Illustrated by Rita Radney

Long ago there lived a handsome young man who was the son of a chieftain. The young man's name was Kia-Tumba Ndala. All of the young women in the village watched Kia with smiles and bright eyes. He was the most adored bachelor around.

Soon the time came for Kia to choose a bride. However, he wanted only to marry the daughter of the Sun and the Moon, not a woman of the Earth as everyone expected. Kia's father, Kimanaueze, thought his son's wish to marry the daughter of the Sun and the Moon was silly.

"How will you get all the way up to heaven to propose to her?" asked Kimanaueze.

But Kia stuck with his wish, answering, "We'll see. But I'm not marrying anyone else."

As word spread about Kia's wish, the villagers began to think maybe he was under a strange spell. But Kia was so determined that he wrote a marriage proposal asking Lord Sun for his daughter's hand.

The problem was, how would he get it to heaven when he could not get up there himself? Kia went to Antelope and asked if she could deliver it, but she said it was too far. Kia asked Hawk and then Vulture, but despite both of them having wings, they turned Kia down. Hawk and Vulture said that they could only make it half of the way.

Frog overheard Kia's request and offered to take the letter to heaven. Kia could not see how Frog would be able to do it, but he gave him the letter anyway.

What Kia did not know was that Frog lived near the well from which Lord Sun and Lady Moon's helpers fetched water every day when they came down from heaven. Frog planned to stow away in their buckets and ride up to heaven and back without ever being noticed.

As planned, Frog made it to heaven hidden in a water bucket. When the time was right, he jumped out of the bucket, put Kia's letter on the kitchen table, and went back to hide. Soon Lord Sun came in for some water and saw the letter. He read it and was intrigued by the mysterious message.

Frog returned to Earth the same way he had left. He immediately went to tell Kia the good news.

"If you delivered it, then where is the reply?" Kia asked.

"I don't know," said Frog. "But I do know that Lord Sun read it. If you write another letter asking for an answer, I will again deliver it."

So Kia did. And Frog went back to heaven in the same way and left the letter on the table.

Lord Sun read Kia's letter and wrote back. Lord Sun said he would approve the marriage only if Kia came in person and brought a gift.

Kia was overjoyed when Frog returned with this reply. But the problem was again, how would Kia get to heaven?

Kia gave Frog a gift of gold coins to bring to Lord Sun, and Frog went to deliver the gift in his usual way. After Frog arrived, he waited until everyone was asleep, then tiptoed into the daughter's room.

Frog brought with him a magic needle and thread. He gently sewed the daughter's eyes shut. It was magical, so the daughter felt no pain.

When the daughter awoke and could not open her eyes, her worried parents sent messengers down to Earth to ask Doctor Ngombo for advice. Frog got back to Earth first by way of the helpers' bucket, and he raced over to the doctor's hut as fast as he could.

Luckily, the doctor had stepped away. So when Lord Sun and Lady Moon's messengers arrived, Frog hid behind the door and pretended to be the doctor.

Frog told the messengers to send the daughter to Earth for treatment at once. The messengers did as they were told.

When the daughter arrived, Frog snipped the magical thread away, and she could see perfectly! He then took her to Kia's hut. When they met, Kia and the daughter fell in love instantly. Frog, who did not like to be thanked, quickly hopped away. The lovers got married, and everyone was happy!

Oh, Won't You Sit Down?

Who's that yonder dressed in red?
Must be the children that Moses led.
Who's that yonder dressed in white?
Must be the children of the Israelite.

Oh, won't you sit down?
Lord, I can't sit down.
Oh, won't you sit down?
Lord, I can't sit down.
Oh, won't you sit down?
Lord, I can't sit down,
'Cause I just got to heaven,
Goin' to look around.

WILEY AND THE HAIRY MAN

Adapted by Karima Amin
Illustrated by David Cooper

iley listened to his mama. She knew all about the Tombigbee River swamp and the terrible Hairy Man who lived there. Wiley's mama told him his papa had fallen into the river and was never seen again.

"If you go into the swamp, take your hound dogs," his mama warned. "The Hairy Man's scared of them."

One day, Wiley went into the swamp to cut some poles for the hen roost. While he was working, his dogs ran off after a wild pig. Wiley was alone when he saw the Hairy Man coming toward him, carrying a sack. He had bulging eyes and big, sharp, yellow teeth. Stiff hair covered most of his body, and his toes looked like cow hooves.

Wiley dropped his axe and climbed a tree. "Why are you up in that tree?" the Hairy Man asked.

"Mama told me to stay away from you," Wiley replied. "What do you have in that sack?"

"Nothing . . . yet," said the Hairy Man.

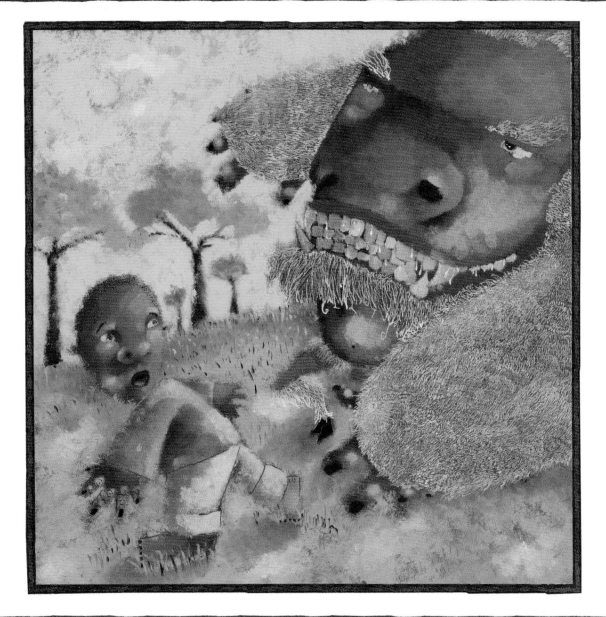

Then he picked up Wiley's axe and began to chop at that tree. He was chopping fast! Wiley began to yell, "Fly, wood chips, fly! Go back into your same old place!" Those wood chips did just what Wiley said and went right back to their places in the tree trunk.

The Hairy Man chopped faster. Then Wiley heard his dogs and hollered, "Here, dogs!" The Hairy Man tossed that axe and ran off through the swamp.

Back home, Wiley's mama said, "I know how to get rid of that Hairy Man. Next time you see him, say, 'Hello, Hairy Man. I hear you're the best conjure man around.'"

Wiley's mama continued, "A conjure man knows magic. Ask him to change himself into something big. Then ask him to change into something little. When he does, grab him and put him in his sack. Then throw it into the river."

The next time Wiley had to go into the swamp, he tied his dogs up at home. When Wiley saw that Hairy Man, he said, "Hello, Hairy Man."

Then he asked the Hairy Man to change himself into a giraffe, an alligator, and a possum. When the Hairy Man changed into a possum, Wiley grabbed him, put him in the sack, and threw him into the river.

Then on the way home, Wiley saw . . . THE HAIRY MAN! Wiley climbed a tree — fast! "Hah! I changed myself into the wind and blew my way out of the sack," said the Hairy Man. "Come down here. I'm hungry!"

"Can you make things disappear, like the rope around my pants?" Wiley asked.

"I can make all the rope in the county DISAPPEAR!" growled the Hairy Man, and that is exactly what he did.

Wiley hollered, "Here, dogs!" The rope that held the dogs back home disappeared, and the dogs chased the Hairy Man away. When Wiley returned home, his mama said, "You tricked the Hairy Man twice. If we can do it one more time, we'll be rid of him forever." Wiley's mama sat down and closed her eyes to think. Wiley's mama had conjure magic, too!

For protection, Wiley crossed a broom and an axe over the window. Then he built a fire in the fireplace. His mama asked for a piglet from the pen. She put it in Wiley's bed under a quilt, and Wiley hid in the loft.

The dogs suddenly started to chase some wild animals, and then Wiley heard the Hairy Man on the roof. The hot chimney kept him outside, but at the front door the Hairy Man hollered, "Wiley's mama, if you don't give me your baby boy, I'll destroy everything you own!"

"I'll give the baby to you, if you promise never to come back," Wiley's mama offered. The Hairy Man promised, and Wiley's mama opened the door, pointing to Wiley's bed. The Hairy Man rushed in and discovered a piglet under the quilt. "This is a baby pig!" he roared.

Wiley's mama declared, "I never said which baby I'd give you." A very angry Hairy Man grabbed the piglet and ran off into the swamp. Wiley and his mama danced for joy!

And they never saw the Hairy Man again.

THIS TRAIN

This train is bound for glory,
This train.
This train is bound for glory,
This train.
This train is bound for glory,
Don't ride nothin' but the good and holy.
This train is bound for glory,
This train!

This train don't pull no extras,
This train.
This train don't pull no extras,
This train.
This train don't pull no extras,
Don't pull nothin' but the midnight special.
This train don't pull no extras,
This train!

DRUM SONG

Adapted by Vincent F.A. Golphin
Illustrated by Mark Galbreath

tikuma wanted to prove he was a man. His father and two older brothers planted, weeded, and harvested the crops. They fed, herded, and milked the cows. Ntikuma was only thirteen, so he had to help his mother around the house.

One morning his father called out, "Kuma," which is what everyone called Ntikuma, since no one used full names. "Come out here." The boy went into the yard. "Your brothers and I are going to the city to sell vegetables," the father said. "You must help your mother with the farm."

"Oh yes, Father," Kuma said with glee. "Don't worry. I will be glad to help."

"You will have to care for the cows and chickens and do what your mother says," said Kuma's father.

"I'll do a good job," Kuma said. Kuma worked for more than two weeks from dawn until night. His mother was pleased.

Then one day she handed Kuma two shiny pennies. "Get peas for supper from the village market," she said. Off he ran.

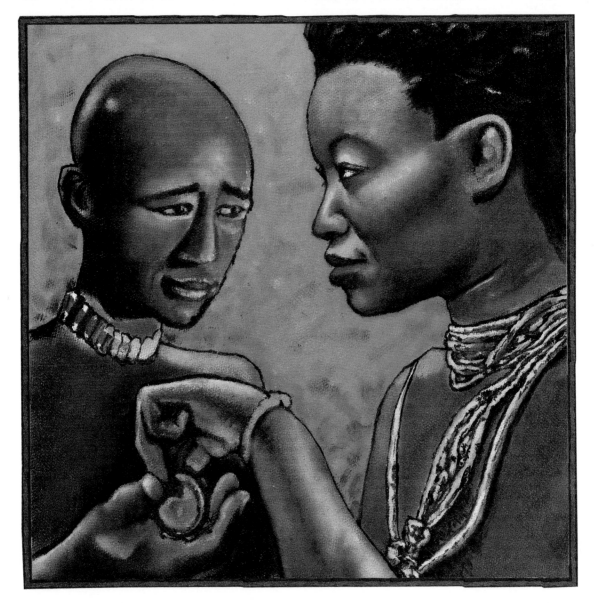

Kuma had been to the outdoor market many times, but never alone. The sellers' booths looked bigger. The shoppers' colorful clothes seemed brighter. The food smells were stronger. As Kuma strolled past the people and goods, the whole place sounded louder.

"Buy my bread!" an old woman yelled.

"Pots and pans!" a man called out.

"Fresh greens and fruit!" shouted another.

One sound rose above the others – *Be-bong, bong*! The wonderful beat filled Kuma's ears. *Be-bong, bong*! It touched his heart. *Be-bong, bong*! He ran toward the beautiful sound. *Be-bong, bong*!

The sound came from a booth, but Kuma was too short to see. A crowd of dancing shoppers blocked Kuma. The boy pushed through to a space filled with more drums. Tall as a horse and short as a pup, round as a barrel and shaped like a cup, the drums created so much joy and excitement.

A salesman pounded the drum song. Kuma watched his hands go up and down. The man laughed. "You like my drum? Here, you try!" said the man, as he handed the boy a small drum. Kuma played and forgot the peas.

"How much?" he yelled to the seller.

"Six pennies today!" the man shouted.

Kuma was saddened. "I only have two," he said.

"No, six!" the salesman shouted. Kuma sadly kept playing. The salesman watched for a long time. "You play very well," he said to the boy. "Give me the two pennies."

Kuma's face lit up. He quickly closed the deal and started home. He forgot the dancers and the peas. The boy just played until he heard the shoppers following him and dancing. "Oh no!" Kuma said, as he remembered the peas. "I've disobeyed my mother. I broke the promise to my father. What should I do?"

"Keep playing!" several dancers shouted. "We love the drum song!"

Be-bong, bong! Kuma kept playing as he slowly walked home to beg forgiveness. Kuma's mother heard the crowd outside the house. "Where are the peas?" she asked as Kuma played the drum and the people danced.

"I'm sorry," Kuma said. "I forgot and spent the money on this drum. I know it was wrong, but I loved the sound."

Suddenly, Kuma's father and brothers stepped out of the crowd. "What is going on?" asked Kuma's father.

"Oh Father, I'm sorry," said Kuma as he continued to play. "I went to the market and spent the food money on this drum."

Kuma's father said, "The song is beautiful, but what will we eat?"

"I'll share my vegetables," said a dancer. Another one offered a pig. Others gave bread and other foods. The family and their new friends had a feast. Everyone ate and danced.

"You've done well, young man," Kuma's mother and father said to Kuma as the crowd left. "Very well done!"

Swing Low, Sweet Chariot

Swing low, sweet chariot,
Coming for to carry me home.
Swing low, sweet chariot,
Coming for to carry me home.

I looked over Jordan, and what did I see,
Coming for to carry me home?
A tall band of angels coming after me,
Coming for to carry me home.

If you get there before I do,
Coming for to carry me home.
Tell all my friends I'm coming too,
Coming for to carry me home.

I'm sometimes up, I'm sometimes down,
Coming for to carry me home.
But still my soul feels heavenly bound,
Coming for to carry me home.

ANNIE CHRISTMAS

Adapted by Karima Amin
Illustrated by Pernell Johnson

That Annie Christmas was really something else. She was stronger than any man, but all woman! Although she lived more than one hundred years ago, people in and around New Orleans still love to tell stories about Annie Christmas.

Annie stood seven feet tall and weighed more than two hundred and fifty pounds. She had smooth black skin, a booming voice, and a good heart. While working on the docks on the Mississippi River, she dressed like a man. For parties, Annie wore a dress made of gleaming red satin. She also wore her favorite pearl necklace and always had on a hat with a red turkey feather.

Annie owned her own flat-bottomed keelboat, and on it she hauled cotton, flour, and lumber. Sometimes she carried passengers whose eyes popped in amazement as they watched her move heavy loads through the water. Annie was a widow, but she had twelve big, strong, handsome sons, all born on the same day! Annie Christmas loved her work, but she always said, "My boys are my joy!"

One day, Annie got all dressed up for a fun trip on her boat. She asked some lady friends to join her on her trip. They sailed up the Mississippi River, stopping at river towns along the way.

At each town, a lady friend would leave Annie, who soon found herself all alone. When a fancy paddle-wheeler steamboat came along, Annie decided to get on board. She could hear happy music and lots of laughter coming from that grand boat.

When Annie arrived on board, she saw several men and women dressed in elegant clothes and having a party. Annie had a wonderful time eating, drinking, and dancing, and also gambling and arm-wrestling with the men.

Then it happened. Suddenly, the sky filled with black storm clouds, the wind began to rise, and a hard rain began to fall.

With the storm in full force, that big fancy steamboat was in trouble.

When the captain decided to take a shortcut through a narrow channel, Annie told him not to do it.

She yelled above the roar of wind and water, "If you go that way, you'll get stuck in a sandbar for sure! Let me help!"

The captain scowled, "I'm the captain of this here boat! Leave me, woman!"

When Annie saw that things were getting worse, she begged the passengers to climb onto her keelboat. Everyone, except the captain, did as she asked.

With muscles straining, Annie poled her boat to safety. They say that when she got her boat back to New Orleans from Natchez, Annie wasn't even breathing hard, and she had plenty of strength to spare.

Annie was a hero! The people couldn't stop talking about her strength and bravery.

"Annie is the greatest! Annie is the best!" said all of the passengers who Annie saved.

A few days later, Annie lay in her bed, not feeling very well. That heroic trip she made from Natchez to New Orleans had put a strain on her heart.

When Annie died, her twelve sons laid her out in her red satin dress and her hat with the red turkey feather. They made sure that she wore her favorite necklace, too.

The sons then placed Annie in a coal-black coffin lined with black satin. The coffin was placed on a coal-black hearse pulled by six coal-black horses.

Annie's sons walked alongside the hearse, six on each side, down to the New Orleans riverfront. That night, under a full moon, they placed the coffin on a coal-black barge and sent it out to sea.

Some people say that Annie's sons floated on that barge with their mother.

I believe those who say the sons stood on the shore, with a prayer on their lips, watching the barge in the moonlight until it vanished forever.

John Henry

When John Henry was a little baby,
Sittin' on his momma's knee,
He picked up a hammer
And a piece of steel
And said, "This hammer'll be
The death of me,
Lord, Lord, this hammer'll be
The death of me."

John Henry said to the foreman,
"Bring that thirty-pound hammer 'round.
Thirty-pound hammer
With a nine-foot handle,
Gonna beat your steam drill down,
Gonna beat your steam drill down."

JOHN HENRY

Adapted by Vincent F.A. Golphin
Illustrated by Christopher B. Clarke

The West was full of open spaces when the C & O Railroad was new. Steel tracks had to be laid through the rugged West Virginia mountains so settlers could come through. Over hills and down deep valleys, many men worked a plan that birthed the thrilling legend about a steel-drivin' man.

"Keep on drivin'!" yelled the foreman. Mile after mile, the workers did race. For every section of rail set down, men hammered spikes to hold them in place.

One by one, workers lifted sledges and slammed the nails on the head. "Come on, keep up with John Henry," the foreman always said.

With skin as dark as midnight, shoulders wide as two trees, John Henry stood nearly seven feet tall. His voice carried a mile on the breeze.

He used a 30-pound hammer, nailing track faster than a four-man crew. The workers at Big Bend Mountain said he was the best they ever knew.

John Henry hammered long steel rods, piercing the red shale mountain wall. He could drill a dynamite hole forty feet when the foreman gave a call.

"Come over here, John Henry," the foreman said, "and make us another hole." The strong-armed giant drove that steel like he was digging for silver or gold.

The blaster lit the fuses, and the workers ran and hid. After the big explosion, they hauled rocks away on a skid. As a thousand men carved the mountain for $1.25 a day, the railroad owner told the foreman, "That's more men than we need to pay."

One day in 1870, the foreman told the workers about the C & O's plan. "We're going to use this steam engine drill," he said. "It's faster than a man. We've got to cut the Big Bend Tunnel, the biggest ever done. No man can drive these rods fast enough, not even a steel-drivin' one."

The angry workers shouted at the foreman. One after another asked him, "Why?" John Henry yelled, "Boss, a man never knows what he can do until he gives it a try."

"Bring the steam-powered drill closer," said the foreman to the engineer. The men let out a rousing cheer, and John Henry showed no fear.

The steam drill slammed one rod then another into that mountain face. John Henry's hammer answered each stroke to match the grueling pace.

Two or three hours soon passed, and people wondered how big John Henry would last.

The blaster set the charges after every rod was drawn. Explosions roared across the valleys as the race went on and on.

"Keep that steel a-comin'," John Henry said with a grin. The side of the mountain opened right up, and the steam drill moved on in.

John Henry drove those rods all day Monday, hammered away on Tuesday, too. When the rooster crowed on Wednesday, the race was finally through.

The steam drill cleared a mile-long path, slammed 130 rods. John Henry tunneled through a mile and a half, and won against all odds.

The workers all walked right down the shaft past the defeated iron drill. They marveled at what a man could do with the power of his will.

"He's a steel-drivin' man!" every worker yelled out. "Look, see what he has done!" Up on the other side of the mountain, John Henry smiled in the blazing sun.

The foreman told John Henry, "I'm sorry that I pushed such a plan. I should'a known that no engine could whip a steel-drivin' man."

"A man never knows just what he can do," a tired John Henry said. Then he heaved a long sigh and fell to the ground. John Henry now was dead.

He is buried beside Big Bend Mountain, right where the east-west tunnels cross. The spot has a statue and a plaque that tells of the hero who was lost.

OVER MY HEAD

Over my head I hear music in the air.
Over my head I hear music in the air.
Over my head I hear music in the air.
There must be a God somewhere.

Over my head I hear singing in the air.
Over my head I hear singing in the air.
Over my head I hear singing in the air.
There must be a God somewhere.

Over my head I see trouble in the air.
Over my head I see trouble in the air.
Over my head I see trouble in the air.
There must be a God somewhere.

Over my head I see glory in the air.
Over my head I see glory in the air.
Over my head I see glory in the air.
There must be a God somewhere.

HISTORY
AND BIOGRAPHY

INTRODUCTION

In this section we celebrate the African-American men and women who have made great contributions to our nation and to the world. You will learn of the important role African-Americans played in the development of the United States as well as the role they continue to play in the present day.

You will experience how African-American artists, writers, craftsmen, and musicians gave America some of its most distinctive art forms. You will read about a people who unleashed their emotions and ideas about life, and in the process made life more enjoyable for everyone.

African-American teachers, doctors, scientists, military heroes, sports figures, explorers, and others have contributed so much to society. This section will inspire you, make you feel special, and plant hope for the future. It will make you want to learn more about this exceptional group of people and perhaps inspire you to achieve great things in your life.

—*Professor Gwendolyn Battle Lavert, Indiana Wesleyan University*

DOCTORS
AND EDUCATORS

Written by S. Pearl Sharp
Illustrated by Rodney Pate

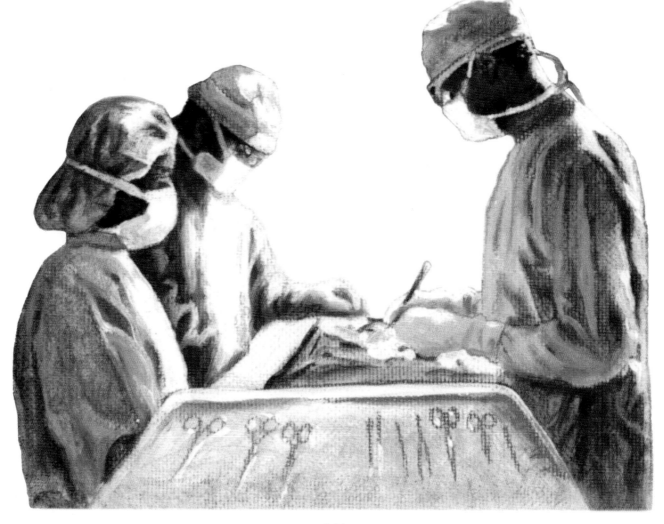

Imagine being arrested just for doing your homework! In America during the early 1800s this was a real possibility. Slave owners began to fear the power of an educated slave, so laws were passed to keep people from teaching any slave to read or write.

But many slaves thought education was worth the risk, because it eventually could lead to their freedom. They often would try to learn at night when their chores were done. One of the things they used for their lessons was Freedom's Journal, an anti-slavery newspaper edited by John Russworm, who was a free African-American.

Many of the Africans who were brought to America as slaves were descendants of tribes who had built some of the world's most important learning centers, such as the empire of Songhay and the libraries of Timbuktu. Sometimes slaves received just a little education from their masters or religious organizations, such as the Quakers. But free black men, like John Russworm, were allowed to attend school. In 1826 he became one of the first African-American college graduates in the United States.

Many other African-Americans made education their most important goal. Carter G. Woodson, born in 1875, had to skip school in order to help support his family. But he taught himself to read and went on to earn degrees from several colleges. Dr. Woodson became the leading author and teacher of African-American history at the time.

In 1926 Dr. Woodson introduced Negro History Week to highlight the contributions made by African-Americans to the development of the United States. The week eventually grew into Black History Month, which our nation celebrates every February.

One of Dr. Woodson's many friends was Mary McLeod Bethune. She started a school in Florida with just a few dollars and five students. Over the years the school grew and grew and eventually became Bethune-Cookman College.

Bethune and Dr. Woodson earned widespread respect for their excellent work in education. In honor of their many contributions, the U.S. Post Office featured each of them on postage stamps.

Educators and other scholars, like Dr. Woodson, earn the title of Doctor (Ph.D.) by mastering a certain area of knowledge. A medical doctor (M.D.) takes care of our health, and many do research to find cures for diseases.

We benefit every day from doctors who do scientific work to benefit our health or create new products. The first blood bank, where donated blood is stored, was created by Dr. Charles R. Drew, an African-American. The blood that is donated at these banks is used to save lives during surgery, when a patient needs extra blood to replace the amount he or she has lost.

Black scientists throughout the years have developed systems to help people grow more food, prevent waste products from hurting the earth, increase energy sources, and even make a longer-lasting house paint.

Scientists often work for years to find the solution to a certain problem or a cure for a disease. When they succeed, it is called a "breakthrough." That is, they have moved beyond what was previously known and discovered something new.

Dr. Keith Lanier Black is an African-American surgeon and teacher who performs nearly 200 brain-tumor operations each year. He also is using the latest technology as he tries to develop a cure for brain tumors.

Another African-American, Dr. Ben Carson, was a poor student until his mother insisted that he read more and write small reports on his books. This homework changed his life, and he became excited about learning.

Dr. Carson is now a successful surgeon, professor, and author of three books. In one of Dr. Carson's most difficult surgeries, he successfully separated twins who were born joined together.

Some well-known African-Americans throughout the years have been both doctors and educators. Dr. Walter Massey was a wiz in physics. He found a way to use liquid helium to slow down the motion of atoms so that scientists could study their activity. Later on, Dr. Massey became a college president and also headed the American Association for the Advancement of Science.

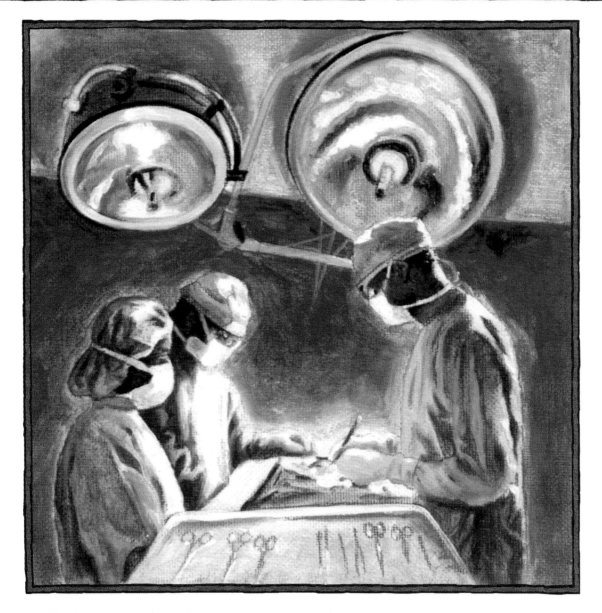

African-American doctors and researchers also have made many contributions to NASA, the National Aeronautics and Space Administration, since the beginning of the space program. Dr. Patricia Cowings from the University of California has done work for NASA for more than 20 years. Among other things, she helped develop ways to reduce astronauts' headaches and space sickness during flights.

Christine Darden, who has been with NASA since 1966, is a mathematician and engineer whose work has made spacecraft wings and nose cones safer. Dr. Vance Marchbanks, who is a medical specialist for NASA, developed ways to monitor astronauts' health during space flights. He was responsible for the health of astronaut John Glenn, who made the United States' first manned flight into orbit.

Dr. Robert Shurney, from Tennessee State University, designed the tires for the moon buggy that was used during the Apollo 15 mission that landed on the moon in 1972. And in 1992, Dr. Mae Jemison became the first African-American woman in space. While aboard the space shuttle Endeavor for eight days, she conducted several medical experiments.

African-Americans also have made key contributions to the current information age. They have developed systems that let the memory on your computer expand, and they also have contributed to the creation of very small yet powerful computers. This new technology is being used to help educate and improve the health not only of other African-Americans but of people of all races.

Learning about the past helps us prepare for the future. But what would it be like if you could actually zoom ahead into the future?

If you close your eyes, you can imagine a young slave time-traveling from the 1800s into the 21st Century. He could visit a lab where African-American scientists are preparing for life in space, or enter a classroom where students his age are learning ancient history as well as advanced mathematics.

In this century, as a free and educated African-American, he can be anything he wants to be. Even though he would find computers everywhere, he probably would still want to experience the magic of reading a book.

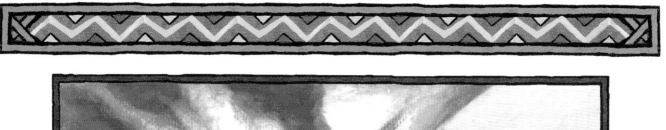

AMAZING GRACE

Amazing Grace!
How sweet the sound,
That saved a wretch like me.
I once was lost,
But now I'm found,
Was blind but now I see.

'Twas Grace that taught
My heart to fear,
And Grace my fears relieved.
How precious did
That Grace appear,
The hour I first believed.

SCIENTISTS AND INVENTORS

Written by Yvonne Shinhoster Lamb
Illustrated by Frank Norfleet

magine a world without traffic lights, elevators, or even something as common as peanut butter. What would life be like with no lawnmowers, refrigerators, or ice cream? In these times, how would millions of people get through the average day without a cellular phone to help them keep in touch with others?

Throughout history, African-American men and women have used their creative talents to improve the lives of people all over the world. Their inventions continue to make life a more healthy and enjoyable experience and also make work less dangerous and more fulfilling.

Back in the 1800s, an African-American named Henry Blair looked for a better way to plant corn and cotton. He went on to invent planting machines that helped to change farming in this country.

In 1834, Blair became the first African-American inventor to be issued a patent. A patent is an official document that gives an inventor the exclusive right to produce and sell his inventions for a certain number of years.

About 50 years later, Sarah Boone made housework a little easier when she created the ironing board. And in 1905, Sarah Breedlove Walker, best known as Madame C.J. Walker, gave women a new way to groom their hair when she invented the straightening comb.

Benjamin Banneker stands out among early inventors. Banneker was born a free man in Ellicott's Mills, Maryland, in 1731. He attended only a few sessions of elementary school and mostly taught himself to read and write.

His studying made a difference. Banneker became a respected mathematician, astronomer, surveyor, and writer. When he was in his early 20s, he became fascinated with a watch that belonged to a friend.

Banneker took the watch apart and put it back together again several times. He borrowed books on geometry and studied them. Then he carved pieces of wood to resemble the watch's gears. Banneker built the first striking wooden clock in colonial America. The clock kept perfect time for many years.

Years later, Banneker became part of a team of surveyors who planned how the streets of Washington, D.C., would be laid out. He also was well-known by scientists throughout the world for his precise predictions of solar eclipses. Banneker also wrote boldly against slavery.

Everyone who enjoys cookies, cakes, and ice cream can say thanks to Norbert Rillieux and Augustus Jackson. Their inventions continue to make life a little sweeter every day. Norbert Rillieux was born in 1806. He attended school in Paris and became an engineer and inventor. Rillieux created a better way for sugar to be made into the white crystals we use today. His inventions in 1846 made it easier to change sugar cane, the plant from which sugar comes, into sugar crystals. This process made sugar easier to use.

Augustus Jackson made and sold custard in New York. He created the first ice cream. As the story goes, Jackson put a pail of custard in a bucket of cracked ice to cool it off. The custard froze. Jackson tasted it and liked it, and so did his neighbors and his customers. He then began selling his ice cream in quart tins for a dollar each.

So many of the inventions by African-Americans have proved useful in everyday life. The inventions helped to make work easier. Shoes and more shoes is what Jan Ernst Matzeliger's invention made possible. He built a machine in the late 1870s that would make up to 700 shoes in one day, compared to 50 made by hand. His invention, called the Lasting Machine, changed the shoe business.

In 1881, Lewis Howard Latimer invented and patented the first electric light bulb with a thin carbon wire. Latimer was an electrical engineer who worked for Thomas Edison, the famous inventor who introduced electric lighting to the world. Latimer also wrote the first textbook on the lighting system used by Edison.

Granville T. Woods and Garrett Morgan thought about safety as they invented dozens of devices. One of Woods' best-known inventions was a system for getting messages from one train engineer to another. His efforts helped to stop train accidents. Morgan designed a safety helmet that was used by firemen in the early 1900s, but he is most famous for his invention that is used everywhere, the traffic light.

George Washington Carver developed a mountain of products from the tiny peanut. Carver was born a slave in Missouri in 1861. It wasn't until he was ten years old that he first went to school. Later, he went to college and studied plant life.

In 1896, Carver eagerly accepted an offer at the Tuskegee Institute in Alabama to lead its new department of agriculture. Carver made history while he was there. His experiments on peanuts, sweet potatoes, and soybeans led to products that improved life for millions of people.

Carver also changed the bleak picture of agriculture in the South. He gave cotton farmers hope with new crops that could earn them more money. Carver created more than 400 products from the peanut and sweet potato, and other items came from Carver's work with soybeans and pecans.

Carver either invented or developed new forms of many products. Among these were peanut butter, bleach, shampoo, flour, coffee, house paint, printing ink, cheese, and soap.

African-American scientists have made many wonderful contributions to the health and welfare of people throughout the world. Dr. Ernest Just conducted research in the 1930s that changed our understanding of how a cell works. Dr. Louis Tompkins Wright developed a special way to vaccinate people against smallpox, which did away with scarring on the skin.

One scientist who stands out for his study of blood is Dr. Charles R. Drew. He was an outstanding athlete, surgeon, scientist, and teacher. He discovered that blood plasma could be stored longer than whole blood and then be ready for use in medical emergencies. Plasma is the liquid part of blood. It is blood without the cells.

Dr. Drew's work helped to save thousands of lives when blood plasma was used by the British during World War II to save wounded soldiers. He also helped to set up blood banks, which we use today to store blood for times of need.

Dr. Drew's great contributions to the world will never be forgotten. Neither will the great work of the many other African-American scientists and inventors.

O Brothers, Don't Get Weary

O brothers, don't get weary,
O brothers, don't get weary,
O brothers, don't get weary,
We're waiting for the Lord.

We'll land on Canaan's shore,
We'll land on Canaan's shore,
When we land on Canaan's shore,
We'll meet forever more.

O brothers, don't get weary,
O brothers, don't get weary,
O brothers, don't get weary,
We're waiting for the Lord.

WRITERS
AND ARTISTS

Written by Tara Jaye Morrow
Illustrated by Gino L. Morrow II

ow powerful are words? Great civilizations were built upon them. Wars have been prevented and people have fallen in love because of words. The words of African-American authors have made a major contribution to American and world literature. These authors have written history books, plays, poems, music, movie scripts, and more.

In the beginning, much of their work was about slavery and the hardships they faced in America, but they also wrote a great deal about religion, music, family, and the dreams that belong to every human being. This is important because these are the things that have put a smile on many faces in good times and bad.

Many African-American writers have won prestigious awards for their powerful work. They will always be loved for the sometimes emotional but always magical journey we take every time we read their words.

Phillis Wheatley was born in 1753 in Africa. At age seven, she became the slave of a wealthy Boston family.

The family taught Wheatley how to read and write English, and even though she never went to school, she also learned Greek and Latin. Wheatley was a great writer, and there were two things she wrote about most — the experience of being a black woman in America, and Christianity. One of her most famous pieces was a letter to the students at the University of Cambridge in England. Wheatley was the first African-American writer in America to gain recognition for her work, and her life was an inspiration to future generations.

Zora Neale Hurston was born in 1891 in Notusulga, Alabama, but she claimed Eatonville, Florida, as the place of her birth. She wrote stories, novels, and folklore in addition to an autobiography. Hurston was more than a writer, though. Some considered her to be a scientist and an anthropologist as well. Her most loved book is *Their Eyes Were Watching God*. This novel is about Janie Crawford, a woman who decides to live and love as she sees fit, even though her small town does not agree with her choices. Zora Neale Hurston died in 1960, but her work gets more popular and her legacy shines brighter as time goes by.

The writer Paul Laurence Dunbar was born June 27, 1872, in Dayton, Ohio. His mother was a former slave who told him of her struggles in the South. These stories later appeared in his poems. Dunbar wrote as often as possible. His first book of poems was called *Oak and Ivy*, and his second, *Majors and Minors*, won the favor of critics across the country. That is when Paul Laurence Dunbar really became famous. He also was a teacher and wrote fiction, short stories, and four novels in addition to his poems.

Langston Hughes, who is sometimes called "the poet laureate of the negro race," was born in Joplin, Missouri, on February 1, 1902. In 1921, Hughes left the Midwest to go to school in New York. The year before, he published "The Negro Speaks of Rivers," one of his most famous poems.

Hughes' writing talent developed further during the Harlem Renaissance, a time when African-American artists of every type made their mark on America. In a 1943 column of the *Chicago Defender* newspaper, Hughes introduced Jesse B. Semple, or "Simple," one of the most beloved creations of his career.

Henry Ossawa Tanner was born in 1859 in Allegheny, Pennsylvania. Tanner decided to become a painter at age thirteen after he saw an artist working in a park near his home. He attended the Pennsylvania Academy of Fine Arts in 1879, but he was not treated very nicely because he was African-American. So he went to study in Paris, where he was respected as a great artist. He painted about faith and hope and feelings all people could relate to. Tanner has since been honored in many exhibitions in the United States and France.

Romare Bearden was born in 1914 in Charlotte, North Carolina, but he spent much of his childhood in Harlem, New York. Bearden remembered having artists and musicians at his house all the time. That is how he became a huge blues and jazz fan, and he started working his love of music into his art.

Bearden went to school at Columbia University in New York City and earned his degree in mathematics. He never had a formal art education, but that did not stop him from following his heart. He used his awesome talent and his perspective of life to achieve a booming career in painting.

Bearden's work has been highly admired for its rhythm, beauty, and unique sense of color.

Selma Burke was a sculptor and a teacher who was born in 1900 in Mooresville, North Carolina. She started sculpting with clay from the riverbed near her home and made figures and objects from the clay. Selma's work dates back to the Harlem Renaissance, and she traveled and studied under several famous artists. In 1943, she won an international competition and was chosen to design a portrait of President Franklin D. Roosevelt. She also designed a dime, which is held by Jacob Lawrence in the drawing on the facing page.

At age 82, Jacob Lawrence was considered the most widely praised African-American artist of the 20th century. He was born in Atlantic City, New Jersey, in 1917. When Lawrence and his family later moved to Harlem, New York, his mother enrolled him in an after-school arts program. There he experimented with many different types of art. He used his canvas to make many bold, brightly colored statements on freedom, dignity, struggle, and daily life among African-American people.

In 1970 Lawrence was the first artist to win the Spingarn medal from the National Association for the Advancement of Colored People. He also was a professor and the head of an art department.

There is an old saying that goes, "A picture is worth a thousand words." So when we look at the beautiful pictures created by African artists, we might have enough words to write a book!

The paintings, drawings, and sculptures they created are not only nice to look at, but they often represented a part of daily living and ceremonial rituals. Wood, bronze, ivory, gold, metal, cloth, and copper were some of the materials used as symbols of emotional expression. African art has been a way to record history and often has served as a visual solution to certain problems.

African-Americans continue to use their art and their words to tell stories and to show others where they have been, where they are, and where they are going. Whatever the purpose, art reminds us how beautiful life can be.

O This Ol' Time Religion

O this ol' time religion,
This ol' time religion,
This ol' time religion,
It's good enough for me.

It was good for the prophet Daniel,
It was good for the prophet Daniel,
It was good for the prophet Daniel,
It's good enough for me.

It will take me home to heaven,
It will take me home to heaven,
It will take me home to heaven,
It's good enough for me.

EXPLORERS
AND ASTRONAUTS

Written by Yvonne Shinhoster Lamb
Illustrated by Alex Bostic

or centuries, African-Americans have dreamed of discovering new and distant lands. Some achieved their goals. Their bravery and determination helped them fulfill their dreams.

Both Matthew Alexander Henson and Mae Jemison pushed themselves to continue their journeys even when the roads ahead proved difficult. Henson and others in his group fought the bitter cold and icy stretches of land to reach their destination — the North Pole. Jemison studied and trained hard so she would be prepared to board a space shuttle and travel into space.

Other African-American explorers and astronauts have blazed trails as well. Their efforts have contributed to building the United States into the strong nation that it is today. Their adventurous spirits inspire us all.

In early America, people of African ancestry played important roles in opening the West as trappers, traders, and scouts. Among them were James Beckwourth, John Baptiste Pointe DuSable, and a man known simply as York.

These men were courageous frontiersmen who helped to shape America during the 1700s and 1800s. In the later part of the 1700s, Jean Baptiste Pointe DuSable brought his extensive knowledge and skills as a merchant, fur trader, and farmer to the Midwest. Around 1773 he built a large trading post near Lake Michigan. Later he added a house, two barns, a mill, a dairy, a bakery, a poultry house, a workshop, and many other buildings. The settlement grew to become the city of Chicago.

York, who was once a slave, went on to become a very important member of the Lewis and Clark expedition of 1803-1806. The expedition members mapped new territory and also brought back important information about Native Americans and various plants, animals, and minerals.

James P. Beckwourth was a mountaineer, a scout, and a pioneer. He also was a successful trapper and trader. He is best known for discovering, in 1850, a safer passage through the Sierra Nevada mountains for those seeking gold nuggets in California. That route is now known as The Beckwourth Trail. He also was one of the founders of Pueblo, Colorado.

Matthew Alexander Henson ran away from his Charles County, Maryland, home shortly after his eleventh birthday. At the age of twelve he became a cabin boy on a ship called the *Katie Hines*. The ship's captain taught Henson geography, mathematics, the Bible, literature, history, and navigation. Young Henson sailed to China, Japan, North Africa, and the Black Sea.

Henson's seafaring skills proved valuable when he joined explorer Robert Peary in 1887 on an expedition to survey a canal route through Nicaragua. Henson and Peary worked together for eighteen years on seven different and dangerous Arctic explorations.

Over the years, Henson learned to speak the language of the native Arctic people. When several others on Peary's expedition gave up, Henson pressed on despite the many hardships. As a result, on April 6, 1909, Henson reached the North Pole just ahead of Peary. Four native Arctic people were the only others present when the United States flag was planted in the ice of the North Pole.

African-Americans have played an important part in space exploration since the 1960s. In 1967, Chicago native Robert H. Lawrence became the first African-American astronaut. Major Lawrence never got to make a trip into space, however, due to an unfortunate training accident in his Air Force jet.

The first African-American to go into space was Guion S. Bluford, Jr., a Philadelphia native. His first mission blasted off from the Kennedy Space Center on August 30, 1983. His space shuttle was the first one to take off and land during the night. Bluford flew into space three other times.

On his very first trip into space in 1985, Frederick Gregory served as the pilot of the space shuttle *Challenger*. In 1989, Gregory was honored when he became the first African-American shuttle commander. He was the leader of the crew on the *Discovery* space shuttle and had to make sure everything went well on the mission.

Gregory, a native of Washington, D.C., also was named the commander on the *Atlantis* space shuttle in 1991.

Bernard A. Harris dreamed of being an astronaut when he was eight years old. As he grew up in Texas, he began working toward his goal. He became a pilot, flight surgeon, scientist, and mission specialist.

In February 1995, Harris made history by becoming the first African-American astronaut to walk in space. At that time he was one of only seven African-American astronauts. He was the payload commander during a ten-day mission aboard the space shuttle *Discovery* when he stepped out and made his historic space walk.

About a year later, Winston E. Scott followed in Harris' gravity free footsteps when he flew aboard the space shuttle *Endeavour*. Scott was on his first mission when he spent nearly seven hours walking in space. During this mission, the crew retrieved a satellite that had been launched from Japan ten months earlier.

Scott's next mission was in 1997 aboard the *Columbia*. During that flight, he suited up and walked in space two more times.

Mae Jemison knew that becoming an astronaut would mean hard work. She knew a person needed to be dedicated, brave, and have the mental toughness necessary to earn the right to wear the suit of a NASA astronaut. Jemison possessed all those qualities and more.

Jemison brought a variety of experiences to NASA when she joined in 1987. She worked as a medical doctor and had spent two-and-a-half years as a medical officer with the Peace Corps in the African countries of Sierra Leone and Liberia. She nourished a love for African and African-American studies, dance, and choreography.

Growing up in Chicago, Jemison was determined not to let any obstacles stop her from pursuing a career in science and technology. Jemison's efforts paid off. On September 12, 1992, she became the first African-American woman to travel into space.

During that flight aboard the space shuttle *Endeavour*, Jemison served as the mission specialist and helped conduct experiments in life sciences and material processing.

FREE AT LAST

Free at last, free at last,
I thank God I'm free at last.
Free at last, free at last,
I thank God I'm free at last.

On my knees when the light passed by,
I thank God I'm free at last.
Thought my soul would rise and fly,
I thank God I'm free at last.

Free at last, free at last,
I thank God I'm free at last.
Free at last, free at last,
I thank God I'm free at last.

POLITICS AND LAW

Written by S. Pearl Sharp
Illustrated by John Ward

For many years in our nation's history, right up to the 1950s, there were places in the United States where African-American and white children were not allowed to eat together in restaurants, play together at the park, or even go to school together.

This was called segregation. While some states passed laws that allowed segregation, the nation's highest court passed a law against it.

Politics is what decides how a country or a group will operate. What a person believes about these activities is also called politics.

A law is a rule made by the government. The national, or federal, government and the state governments are always debating about which group gets to make rules and decisions for the people.

The ongoing debate about school desegregation is a good example. At various times, the military has been called upon to enforce laws that called for African-American and white children to be taught in the same schools.

Laws are passed to protect us from something or to set guidelines for our daily actions. They ensure that such things as the right to vote are not denied.

African-Americans have been involved in every aspect of the development of law and politics from colonial times through the history of the United States. For almost 300 years, from the 1600s through the 1800s, many of the laws that were passed dealt with the issue of slavery.

People decided where slavery was legal, how slaves and runaways were to be treated, and what civil rights were to be given to or denied for African-Americans, including their very freedom.

An important case in 1857 declared that a slave, Dred Scott, was not a citizen and had no rights. The outcome of this case also decided how all other slaves should be treated.

Over the next century the Supreme Court as well as the federal government reversed this decision by creating five different civil-rights acts, which were designed to ensure the basic rights of African-Americans.

These acts affirmed the citizenship of African-Americans, their right to vote and to have equal access to public facilities, and the government's responsibility to become involved in all of these matters.

After slavery ended in the United States there was a short period called Reconstruction when African-Americans were treated as full citizens. African-American men, but not women, won the right to vote for the first time.

Twenty-two African-Americans were elected to the U.S. Congress, where they fought for equality and free public schools. When Reconstruction ended, however, attitudes started to change, and a series of laws known as "Jim Crow" took away most of the rights African-Americans had gained.

African-Americans did not give up. The next generation produced many strong political leaders. One was congressman Adam Clayton Powell, a handsome, flamboyant minister from Harlem, New York. When he began his first term in Washington, D.C., he was not allowed to get a haircut in the Congressional barber shop because it was segregated.

Powell served 11 terms and pushed many controversial laws against discrimination through Congress. In fact, he added anti-discrimination clauses to so many laws that the clauses became known as the Powell Amendments.

Shirley Chisholm worked as a nursery-school teacher before she became the first African-American woman ever elected to the U.S. Congress. In 1972 she became the first African-American woman to run for the U.S. presidency.

Both Powell and Chisholm worked hard to gain civil rights for African-Americans. Do you know what your civil rights are? They include the right to vote, to receive a basic education, to be served in public restaurants, to sit anywhere on public transportation, to earn a fair wage for work, to live safely in your home, to worship as you choose, to express your opinion about issues, and to receive equal treatment under the law.

During the 1950s and 1960s the civil-rights movement developed because African-Americans had been denied these rights for a long time.

Four college students in Greensboro, North Carolina, decided to "sit in" at a restaurant that would not serve any African-American people. Soon, sit-ins were happening all over the United States. Students and citizens of all races came together and set up centers where African-American citizens could safely register to vote.

Law and politics are always changing. About 150 years ago, African-Americans born in the U.S. were not considered citizens. Politics and legal rulings changed until Shirley Chisholm and, a decade later, Reverend Jesse Jackson were able to run for president of the United States. The right to vote is now protected by an amendment to the United States Constitution and two voting-rights acts.

For decades African-Americans were not even allowed to testify in court. But by 1872 things had changed to the point where Charlotte E. Ray became the first African-American woman lawyer in the U.S. Almost a century later, Thurgood Marshall, who had been a civil-rights lawyer, was appointed to the U.S. Supreme Court. Many African-American attorneys today are among the most skilled lawyers in the U.S.

Laws now protect the rights of African-Americans to vote, travel, buy homes, and use public facilities. The process has been long, from the days of Dred Scott to the work of the great civil-rights leader Dr. Martin Luther King, Jr., up to the present day. Dr. King dedicated his life to securing basic rights for every African-American, and many people honor Dr. King by celebrating his birthday every January 15th. But each of us can actively take part in making the world a better place.

Attorney Marion Wright Edelman was very concerned about the large number of children living in poverty, so she used her skills to create the Children's Defense Fund. This organization protects the interests of children. Mrs. Edelman chose this work because she believes that if you do not like the way the world is, you should change it one step at a time. She became part of the solution.

Maybe there is something in your community that needs changing — a dangerous corner that needs a traffic light, or a vacant lot that could become a nice park. Just remember, you are never too young to bring things to the attention of your local leaders or lawmakers. You really *can* make a difference.

Joshua Fought the Battle of Jericho

Joshua fought the battle of Jericho,
Jericho, Jericho.
Joshua fought the Battle of Jericho,
And the walls came tumbling down.

You may talk about your kings of Gideon,
You may talk about your men of Saul,
But there's none like good old Joshua
At the battle of Jericho.

Straight up to the walls of Jericho
He marched with spear in hand.
"Go blow that ram's horn," Joshua cried,
"For the battle is in my hand."

The ram horns began to blow,
And the trumpets began to sound.
And Joshua commanded, "Now children, shout!"
And the walls came tumbling down.

MILITARY HEROES

Written by Nicole Blades
Illustrated by Derek Blanks

The military has played a vital role in American history. Thousands of African-Americans, both slaves and free men, have served their country in the military, but history books often have not recognized them for their major contributions.

The United States won its independence from Britain after many years of battle during the American Revolution, which ended two centuries of British rule. Crispus Attucks was a runaway slave in Boston, and in 1770 he became a hero of the Revolution when he led a rebellion, later called the Boston Massacre, against British troops. He was killed, along with other protestors, by British soldiers.

Five thousand free African-American men fought for America in the Revolutionary War. There was even one woman named Deborah Sampson who fought disguised as a man.

Some slaves were sent into battle in their owners' place, and they earned their freedom when they enlisted in the Continental Army. After the war, however, the U.S. Congress barred African-Americans from joining the military.

The Civil War is significant because it is the only war in our nation's history that pitted Americans against each other. The Union, or North, battled against the Confederates, or South. The country was divided mainly over the issue of whether to abolish slavery.

Abraham Lincoln, who was president at the time, was against slavery, but the Southern states did not agree with his ideas and plans. Soon, fierce battles broke out between the North's anti-slavery forces and pro-slavery groups in the South.

Even though they often faced severe restrictions, many African-Americans were determined to serve their country during the war. The 54th Regiment of the Massachusetts Volunteer Infantry was the first all-African-American regiment that fought for the North.

In 1863 the 54th regiment became famous for leading an attack on Fort Wagner and also captured the Confederate city of Charleston, South Carolina. Sergeant William Carney of the 54th regiment became the first African-American to be awarded the Congressional Medal of Honor.

During the Civil War over 180,000 African-Americans fought in the Union Army, and more than 33,000 died. The war ended in 1865 with the North defeating the South.

There was a period of change and readjustment, called Reconstruction, which followed the Civil War. New civil-rights laws and a new president, Andrew Johnson, helped to forever change the lives of African-Americans.

Most Southern states soon abolished slavery. In 1865 the government approved the Thirteenth Amendment, which guaranteed freedom for all African-Americans, and a year later Congress passed legislation allowing African-Americans to serve in the military.

In 1866 the first all-African-American military units were formed. The Ninth and Tenth Black Cavalry regiment, nicknamed the Buffalo Soldiers, rode on horses patrolling the Western frontier. Despite the prejudices and extremely harsh living conditions, the Buffalo Soldiers served their country with pride. They became one of the most distinguished and decorated U.S. Army units of all time.

During World War I, Europe was divided, with Germany and Austria-Hungary fighting against Britain, France, and Russia. American President Woodrow Wilson at first wanted the U.S. to remain neutral, but in 1917 America declared war on Germany.

Almost 400,000 African-Americans were drafted into the army or enlisted, but only 50,000 saw actual combat. Many were assigned duties like burying the dead or cleaning mess halls. Some of them were even given the dangerous job of setting off explosives.

One of the most famous African-American soldiers who fought in World War I was Private Henry Johnson. He was part of the 369th Infantry, the first African-American unit of combat troops to land in Europe to aide the French troops.

The 369th was cited for bravery several times, and the French honored the men by awarding them their highest honor, the Croix de Guerre. The commanding officer, General Benjamin O. Davis, was promoted to brigadier general in 1940 and was the first African-American general in the army.

World War II was a turning point for African-Americans in the U.S. military. Despite continuing discrimination, more than one million African-Americans joined the armed forces during this war. Women were given the chance to volunteer, and in 1941 the Women's Army Auxiliary Corps, which later became the Women's Army Corps (WAC), was formed. Nearly 4,000 African-American women proudly served their country as WACs.

In 1942 the U.S. Marine Corps finally started to enlist African-Americans, and Howard P. Perry became the first African-American to join the Marines. Also, the Army Air Corps began to train African-American pilots, resulting in the famous Tuskegee Airmen, the first African-American fighter pilots.

Second Lieutenant Vernon J. Baker should have received the Congressional Medal of Honor for his heroism in 1945, but no African-American soldier received this honor during this period. However, that changed in 1997, when President Clinton awarded the Medal of Honor to Baker and also to six other African-American veterans of World War II.

In 1948 President Harry S. Truman signed the Executive Order. It called for the end of segregation in the U.S. military and equality for all people in the armed services. The Vietnam War became the first battle in American history in which African-Americans were not limited in their duties and served in every area of the military. The Vietnam War came just as the civil-rights struggle was reaching a high point in the Southern states.

At last, African-American men and women were able to climb the ranks in the military based on their merit. They could now be rewarded for their achievements and not be judged simply by their race. In Washington, D.C., the Vietnam Veterans Memorial pays tribute to Americans of all races who gave their lives during the war.

General Colin L. Powell received 11 medals and other decorations for his service in Vietnam. He also was the first African-American chairman of the Joint Chiefs of Staff, which oversees all of the United States' military branches.

African-Americans continue to make history, serving their nation on land, at sea, and in the air.

HE'S GOT THE WHOLE WORLD IN HIS HANDS

He's got the whole world in His hands,
The whole world in His hands,
He's got the whole world in His hands,
He's got the whole world in His hands.

He's got the wind and the rain in His hands,
The wind and the rain in His hands,
He's got the wind and the rain in His hands,
He's got the whole world in His hands.

He's got the tiny little baby in His hands,
The tiny little baby in His hands,
He's got the tiny little baby in His hands,
He's got the whole world in His hands.

He's got everybody in His hands,
Everybody in His hands,
He's got everybody in His hands,
He's got the whole world in His hands.

MUSICIANS

Written by Gino L. Morrow II
Illustrated by Gino L. Morrow II

If you have ever heard the sound of a heartbeat, then you have already begun to learn about the roots of music. When you hear a heartbeat, what do you think about? Perhaps you think about life, or maybe a drum.

When we look at the world around us and see different people in different countries, people of many nationalities and languages and customs, we are able to understand just how unique we are.

But even though we are unique, music is one thing that most people have in common. It seems that no matter where you go, you can find some form of music. It just may be the language of life.

Music is the link that connects us to our ancestral roots in Africa, Australia, the West Indies, North and South America, and every other land in the world. In fact, the music of many of today's famous songwriters and producers can be linked directly to Africa, where some say life began.

African music has influenced all the music of the world, but it may have had the greatest impact on American music.

In Africa, music has long been heard as lullabies, work songs, religious songs, and so on. Despite a great deal of struggle, African people created musical forms that have become stronger and greater, having spread to every corner of the world.

In Spain and other Latin countries, African music had a big influence on new styles of music such as Merengue and Salsa. In the Caribbean, Calypso was influenced by African work songs. Reggae was born when West Indians adopted American rhythm and blues (or R&B) and rock & roll.

In America, African work songs slowly grew into the blues, and Jazz became the first all-American music form. African-American dance music was kept alive through rhythm and blues. Rock music was born when R&B, country music, and ballads were mixed together.

Soul music came from R&B that was mixed with gospel music, and funk and rap music followed. Of course, there would be no musical legacy if it were not for the many musical pioneers who paved the way.

At age six, Marion Anderson (1897-1993) joined the choir of her family's church. She sought to improve her singing, but she was denied access to training because of her race. After high school, Anderson performed in nearly two hundred concerts in Germany and other foreign countries.

She was known and loved for the way she sang classical music and spirituals, but even greater than her voice was her sense of pride and dignity. She overcame racial obstacles that opened doors for countless musicians who followed.

Bessie Smith (1894-1937) was born in Chattanooga, Tennessee, and was one of the finest blues and jazz singers in history. Her recordings from 1923 to 1933 rank among the best in jazz. Until shortly before her death, Bessie's work was almost unknown by white audiences, but African-American audiences bought thousands of her albums. The beauty of her voice transformed simple songs into masterpieces.

Throughout her career she recorded with many jazz greats such as Joe Smith, Fletcher Henderson, James P. Johnson, and Louis Armstrong.

Edward Kennedy Ellington (1899-1974), whose great musical talent earned him the nickname "Duke," was born in Washington, D.C. He was seven years old when he began to play the piano, and at age seventeen he made his professional debut. Ellington was twenty-four when he moved to New York and became a member of the Washingtonians.

Ellington would eventually take over the band and play regularly at the Cotton Club in Harlem. Throughout his career, Duke Ellington enjoyed a worldwide reputation as a great jazz pianist and composer. He is seen by many as the best jazz composer in history.

Richard Penniman, who is known as Little Richard, was born in Macon, Georgia, in 1932. As a composer, singer, and piano player, Richard's energy and talent made him one of the first stars of rock & roll.

During the 1950s, Little Richard recorded a string of hits, including "Tutti Frutti" and "Good Golly, Miss Molly." He sometimes took a break from his music career to serve as an ordained minister in the Seventh-Day Adventist church.

Little Richard's music and flashy performances have had a great impact on other rock performers, including Mick Jagger and the great guitarist Jimi Hendrix.

Teddy Riley, king of "The New Jack Swing," is one of the most influential figures in dance music. Ever since he was small, Teddy has put his heart and soul into music. By age ten, he was playing several instruments and performing in church. He is responsible for more than thirty platinum and multiplatinum records, as well as nine gold records. Riley produced such hits as Bobby Brown's "My Prerogative" and Johnny Kemp's "Just Got Paid," but it was with the vocal group Guy that Riley set the stage for nearly every male R&B performer who followed him.

James Todd Smith's story begins in Queens, New York. As a preschooler, Smith was inspired by his grandfather's jazz albums. By age nine he was already rapping under the name "LL Cool J." At sixteen he released his debut album, "Radio." His 1990 release, "Mama Said Knock You Out," won LL a Grammy award. In 1999 he starred in three movies, "Any Given Sunday," "Deep Blue Sea," and "In Too Deep."

LL Cool J's sitcom "In the House" earned him three Black Image awards. He also opened the Camp Cool J Foundation, a place where all children, rich or poor, could play.

Through the years, many musicians have owed a debt of gratitude to Louis Armstrong, who was born in New Orleans in 1901. Armstrong was known around the world as one of the greatest cornet and trumpet players ever. He also had a distinctive voice that made him a famous scat singer. A scat singer is one who imitates the rhythm of music with sounds rather than words. In 1924, Armstrong, who was living in Chicago, moved to New York to join the Fletcher Henderson band. However, it was after he returned to Chicago that he made recordings that rank among the masterpieces of jazz.

These artists are just a few of many who have paved the way for today's music. They have left a legacy that links us to a rich musical past, one that has seen its share of hardships but still gave birth to musical forms that changed the world. Will the next generation of musicians have the same impact as past greats such as Marion Anderson, Duke Ellington, Jimi Hendrix, and others? Only time will tell.

WHEN THE SAINTS GO MARCHIN' IN

Oh, when the saints go marchin' in,
Oh, when the saints go marchin' in,
Lord, I want to be in that number,
When the saints go marchin' in.

Oh, when they come on Judgment Day,
Oh, when they come on Judgment Day,
Lord, I want to be in that number,
When they come on Judgment Day.

When Gabriel blows that golden horn,
When Gabriel blows that golden horn,
Lord, I want to be in that number,
When he blows that golden horn.

When they go through them Pearly Gates,
When they go through them Pearly Gates,
Lord, I want to be in that number,
When they go through them Pearly Gates.

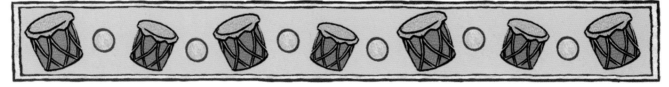

SPORTS HEROES

Written by Robin Ware
Illustrated by Robyn Phillips-Pendleton

Jesse Owens grew up in a poor family in Alabama, but because he earned good grades in school he was able to attend Ohio State University. He competed in track and field events and broke several national records.

Owens was selected to go to the Summer Olympics in Berlin, Germany, in 1936. Adolf Hitler, Germany's ruler at the time, believed that his people were superior to all others in the world, but Jesse Owens showed that Hitler was wrong. Owens won all of his events: the 100-meter and 200-meter dashes, the long jump, and the 4x100-meter relay.

In the early part of the 1900s, two African-Americans stood out in the world of boxing — Jack Johnson and Joe Louis. Johnson was the first African-American heavyweight champion, and he paved the way for other African-American boxers to follow in his footsteps.

One of those was Joe Louis. In 1934 Louis knocked out Jack Kracken to become the heavyweight champion. Louis, also known as "The Brown Bomber," handled himself with class and dignity.

Jackie Robinson was a great baseball player. He hit 137 home runs, stole 197 bases, scored 947 runs, and had a career batting average of .311 over his ten major-league seasons. But statistics cannot measure the great contribution Robinson made to baseball. He was the first African-American to play in the major leagues.

In 1947, with the help of the president of the Brooklyn Dodgers, Robinson made his major-league debut and became a hero in the African-American community. Amid insults, he let his bat, glove, legs, and heart do the talking. He always played hard and always showed the joy and pride he felt. Robinson's actions showed the world that African-Americans could survive anywhere with courage and dignity.

Satchel Paige was a great baseball player and a legend in the Negro Leagues for his fantastic pitching and funny antics. Paige's main goal was to get into the major leagues. In 1948, he finally got his chance when the Cleveland Indians needed an extra pitcher to help them advance to the World Series. Paige joined the team and indeed helped the Indians win the World Series.

Muhammad Ali was one of the best boxers the world has ever seen. He won the world heavyweight title three times, but Ali opened our eyes beyond the ring. He was a man of strong beliefs, and in 1968 he refused to enlist in the Army to go to Vietnam because he did not believe in killing.

Ali had an outgoing personality and always spoke his mind. Today, Ali is well-respected. He showed the world that African-Americans with honorable beliefs can prevail, even when faced with obstacles.

Hank Aaron was a fantastic baseball player. He was an all-around athlete who had a great batting average and could hit for power, run, throw, and field. Aaron did it all, and he finished his career in the mid-1970s with 755 home runs, the highest total in major-league history.

Wilma Rudolph was born in 1940. As a youngster, she was diagnosed with double pneumonia and scarlet fever. Because of this, Rudolph wore leg braces until the age of eleven. She was determined to do well in life, and when she no longer needed braces, she started running in track events.

As a student at Tennessee State University, she qualified for the 1960 Olympics in Rome. Rudolph won the 100-meter and 200-meter dashes and the 4x100-meter relay. She was known as "The World's Fastest Woman."

The late 1950s and 1960s were an exciting period for African-American athletes. With a confidence strengthened by the civil-rights movement, many of these athletes forged ahead in the mission to unite all people and also to give African-Americans a dignified place in society.

Arthur Ashe was born in Virginia in 1943. His father was a tennis instructor, and Arthur came to love tennis from an early age. In 1968, he became the first African-American ever to win the U.S. Open. However, his work outside of tennis was what really made him a hero. He was determined to unite white people and people of color, and he worked to help end inequality in South Africa.

In 1957, Althea Gibson rewrote history when she became the first African-American woman to play in the U.S. Nationals tennis tournament, which she also went on to win.

Gibson had won the French Open in 1956 and also won the Wimbledon tournament in 1957 and 1958. She was able to give African-Americans hope that anything is possible.

Michael Jordan is one of those rare athletes that we see once or twice a century. Gifted with unbelievable athletic ability and charm, Michael was the college player of the year at the University of North Carolina in 1984. He went on to win the NBA title six times with the Chicago Bulls and set countless scoring records. In 1994, seeking another challenge, he became a member of the Chicago White Sox baseball team. Michael struggled as a baseball player but then made a great comeback with the Bulls in 1995. He retired in 1999 and now is trying his talent as the president of the Washington Wizards basketball organization. We have not heard the last from Michael Jordan, the most famous athlete of our time.

The last fifty years have seen great achievements by African-American athletes. They have desegregated sports and have been a force in ending discrimination in America through hard work, grace, leadership, and talent. The new generation continues to build upon these achievements.

12/25/2001

THE END

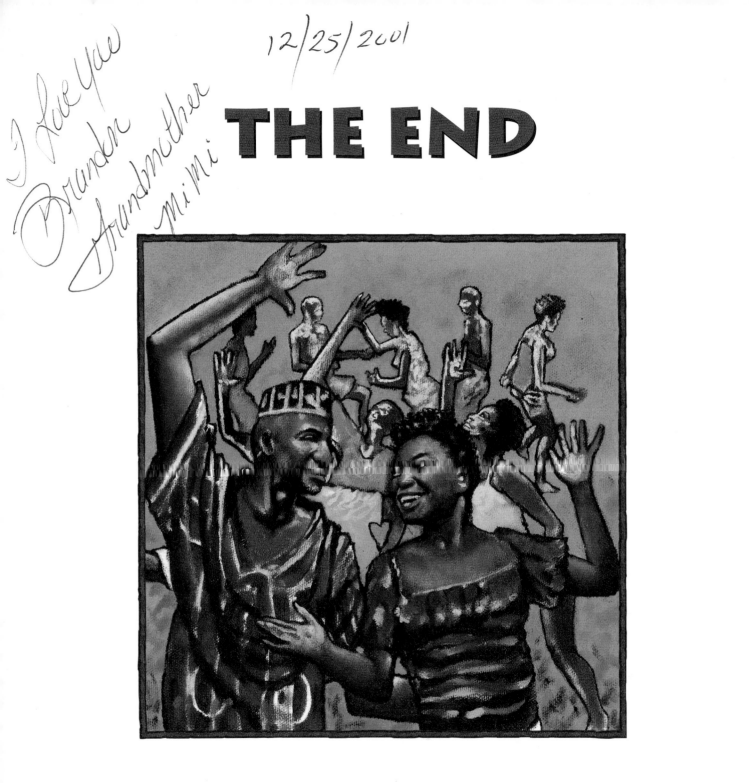